Train Ghost
Ellis J. DelMonte

Late in the day, but still with all my love,
For mum and dad.

Train Ghost
Text copyright © 2006 Ellis J. Delmonte
Cover design by the author © 2006 Ellis J. Delmonte
All rights reserved
ISBN 978-1-84728-392-4

The rights of the author have been asserted

Hawkwood Books 2006
www.lulu.com/hawkwoodbooks

Contents

I   Train Ghost

If she had been asleep, it had been the strangest of sleeps, and if she was now awake, it was the strangest of wakings.

First, there was the silence.

She knew, even before she opened her eyes, that something was wrong. There was neither the familiar pounding of wheels on rails nor the chatter of people around her.

She looked.

No one.

Neither opposite, where mum should have been, nor around her where a hundred passengers should have been.

All gone.

She stood and stared, not understanding.

Outside the windows, terrible to behold, a smothering whiteness. No Cambridge, no London, no land between, just a pure, pristine, bright light that lit the comfortless carriage of her deserted train.

"Mum!" she whispered. "Mum! Are you there?"

No answer.

"Mum! Please! Don't leave me like this!"

Nothing.

She moved into the aisles and walked down, checking each seat.

No one.

Looking through into the next carriage, the same, silent stillness, a taunting, threatening, inexplicable absence of life.

She gripped a door handle, closing her eyes for a moment to remember more clearly.

"My name is Emma Chandler," she said aloud. "I was travelling from Cambridge to London. I…"

Her voice sounded odd in the unnatural silence, and her thoughts appeared jumbled. Even her name seemed distant, hard to catch in the fog of memory. Other images were there, but far away, people she knew and didn't know, a confusion of light and a horrendous sound like an earth-wrecking thunder.

"Mum!" she called into the next carriage, and the one after that, and the one after that, dashing through them, holding down the panic.

Her mother always travelled with her, sometimes dad, too, and her brothers, Calum and little Benjamin. It was a Saturday thing, visiting grandpa and grandma in London.

Wasn't that where she had been going?

"Dad! Cal! Benjy!"

No answer.

How long had she been there? She didn't know. How long might she have to stay there? She feared to think. She sat down on the nearest seat and cried the deepest, most anguished cry of loneliness and fear. She was Emma Chandler, adored by her family, star pupil and star athlete at one of the best schools in the country, clever, talented and full of a life that was rich, ordered and happy. So what had happened that floods of tears were flowing in this nightmare of a train with nothing and no one to give her comfort?

A sound in the silence.

She looked up, dried her eyes and tried to stop the sobbing that obscured the distant whisper.

Unmistakably, a voice.

Emma turned to look, afraid of what she might see, but there was nothing.

She stood, called out,

"Who's there?"

No answer.

She walked up the carriage, listening intently. Her heart beat loudly and each beat touched the whisper.

"Emma! Emma! Emma!"

Her name! Someone was calling her name!

Emma stood still as stone and listened. Yes, no mistake, her name.

"Who's there? Tell me," she asked.

Nothing.

She moved further up the train, into the next carriage.

Empty.

The next.

At the end, shimmering as if disturbed by the faintest of breaths was a small, frail, wispy thing, of human shape yet not human.

Emma stared, uncertain what to think, afraid to speak the only word that came to mind.

Lacking form, it might have been male or female, young or old, impossible to tell, but there was, in the end, no denying the truth.

A ghost.

And it stood there, unmoving, unnerving, murmuring two distinct names, "Emma! Emmy! Emma! ...

2   Emmy Fairchild

Emmy screamed as the train passed overhead. She loved the moment and soaked it up. It filled her with delight, the noise, the power, the danger. Just for a while she felt free of her father and his violent temper, of a school that taught her nothing and of a world that took no interest in her heart filled so uselessly with love. For those fleeting seconds the world was the bridge, the arch, the train, nothing else. Everything was banished by the thunder, swallowing the dark space beneath the level crossing where Emmy spread her arms and bellowed away all her fears and frustrations.

Too soon the train was gone and she was just a frail little girl again, standing in the damp, dark tunnel beneath the railway line, hiding from the world. The quiet after the storm was always strange. She waited and listened as the sound of the train dwindled and died, then scrambled up, all self-conscious, though there was no one in sight.

She saw the train in the distance and waved uncertainly, as if it was part of a fragile friendship. The disappearing train meant reappearing life, and she dreaded it. She was aware of herself again in the daylight, saw her style-less jeans, shabby shirt and torn trainers and blushed. She hated the way she felt, the way she knew she was, an un-cool presence in a brash, cool world.

She peered both ways along the track, but knew the schedules too well, Cambridge to London, London to Cambridge, and no train was due for over an hour.

She checked her watch, big hand, small hand, struggling to decipher the time, decided she was early, and scampered down again into the tiny tunnel, sitting on the stone parapet under the arch, allowing herself a few extra moments of hiding.

She loved the spot, not just because of the trains passing overhead making the whole world shake, but because it was isolated, away from all madness, on the marshes where few people wandered. These were the Walthamstow Marshes, not the more famous Hackney Marshes which lay across the main Lea Bridge Road, a little way away. If you listened carefully, you could hear the cars and lorries, hundreds of them, hurtling along the road, but under the bridge you only heard yourself. It was wonderfully quiet, close to the nature reserve, the wild grasslands, the Lea River, the abandoned greyhound track and the silent Bomb Crater Pond where great reeds grew and moorhens played hide and seek in the murky water. It was the only place she found freedom, where time stood still, a little world of her own.

Time, however, did not stand still. She was getting older, almost thirteen, and she dreaded it because she didn't feel ready. She was a little girl still, and refused the grown up Emmy a passport to the big, bad world. Grown up Emmy had nothing of what the world valued, no riches, no style, no brains, no nothing, so best keep her inside as long as possible. She dreaded what would happen if one day she woke up and the beast was out, all unready and scared, like a rabbit caught in headlights.

She checked her watch again and reluctantly stood up. She both loved and dreaded the run home; she

5

loved the run, dreaded home.

She set off, jogging steadily along the dry mud paths she knew so well, around Bomb Crater Pond, by the river, across the bridge, around the park, pounding the concrete paths, never getting tired. Other kids at school could hardly stand up without getting puffed but Emmy could run for ever. When she ran, she felt free, as if she could circle the world and get back to where she started. She felt part of something much bigger than herself and, more importantly, free of people - the bullies at school and the bully at home. When she was really in tune with the wind, she thought she could hear the voice of her mother telling her why she'd gone and that she'd be back soon. But it was all imagination. Mum had gone and was not coming back.

Emmy stopped in front of the yellow door on the hill, took a deep breath and went in, happy that she'd had a clear run, uncertain of what would happen next.

Her father was moving between rooms when Emmy came in, holding a half filled glass in his hand. Emmy could smell the familiar stench of drink.

"You been down to the railway again?" he asked in a threatening whisper, "I told you not to. Is that why you're late?"

"I ain't late," said Emmy, the excitement of the run dissolving in the face of her father's drunken menace.

She went into the kitchen and her father followed. He waited and watched. Emmy hid her fear. If you showed someone you were afraid they'd go for the kill; people were like that, no more than animals.

"I said six." he muttered. "It's five past."

"Five minutes, dad," said Emmy. "Couldn't 'elp

it."

Her father could have gone either way, into a stormy temper or a quiet moodiness. He fell silent and sat down, his eyes, something of the frightened dog in them, still on her.

"You look like your mum," he said. Emmy didn't answer. Least said, soonest mended. "I bet you cheat like her, too."

"I don't cheat," said Emmy.

She poured some water into a mug stained with grime, then sat down and stared at it, anything but look at her father's bloated red eyes.

"Hmm," he mumbled. "I bet you'd run off and leave me if you could, wouldn't you, Emmy Fairchild, just like your mother?"

Emmy would have done, if she'd had somewhere to go.

"So, tell your dad what you did in school today, Emmy."

He asked not out of interest, but suspicion. She told him the usual lies, how interesting it had all been, how good she was, how the other children liked her, how well she was doing. She could hardly tell him that no one spoke to her because she was the opposite of cool, that she still couldn't read or write properly and that even the sports teachers never looked twice at her because she kept her talent secret, choosing instead just to watch and listen, waiting for that one kind, quiet, helping hand which never came.

"If you ain't tellin' me the truth, Emmy, you know what you'll get, don't you?"

She did, but she lied anyway because lying was the only way.

"You keep your 'ead down," he went on, "Mark my words. Stick it up one inch too far and someone'll smack it down. They always do. You just keep busy and be a good little girl and everything will be fine. No problems. You know that, don't you?"

"I know it, dad."

He leaned over and pinched her cheek, in a friendly way, though there was a clear red mark when he took his hand away.

He reached into his pocket, took out some coins and placed them on the table in front of Emmy.

"Better get some supper," he said, "Fish and chips'll do for me. Get yourself what you want."

Emmy slid the money into her hand, counting the coins. Three pounds. Hardly enough for a feast. Fifteen minutes later she was back, greasy food on greasy plates, eating in silence. When they'd finished, her father sat back and said,

"About you being late."

He just never left off.

"I weren't ..."

"Five minutes is five minutes," he interrupted. "What were you doing?"

"Nuffing. There's nuffing to do."

Her father gave her a piercing look.

"You know what I told you. You play by the railway and I'll punish you, Emmy."

"I weren't."

She wasn't playing, she was just getting away from him.

"I don't want you being late," dad said. "I tell you to be here, you be here."

"It was only five minutes."

Dad gave her a warning look, tapped the table, sniffed and sat back.

"You shouldn't rile me, Emmy. I'm your dad. I do the best I can for you."

Emmy wanted to say so much, but she couldn't find the words. He wouldn't listen anyway.

"I'm off out," he said, getting up and stretching, "You can watch telly till ten, just make sure you're asleep when I get back."

There was little chance he'd be back by ten, unless he caused trouble and someone brought him home. More likely he'd end up in casualty, insulting everyone and causing a rumpus. But she couldn't take the chance. If he came back home and found her awake he'd be trouble. He'd threaten her so loudly that her heart would pound and she'd sweat and tremble.

She didn't watch television but went to her room and closed the door. Her bedroom was a little girl's room, not that of a twelve year old. And untidy, too. The bed hadn't been made since it was bought and her few toys were either old or broken.

She would have read, but words were like broken jigsaws, impossible to put together. She stared at books knowing they held great secrets she would never know, but pictures she understood and gave her clues to meaning.

She drew a lot of pictures, of trains, of the tunnel under the level crossing, of mum, of the marshes and even one of her, Emmy Fairchild, winning a race at the Olympic Games. She wouldn't have shown them to anyone, though, especially the last. She didn't want the world to see how stupid she was.

There was one special one, her favourite.

The Girl in the train.

They'd seen each other for the first time months before, and Emmy would never forget what happened. Coming out of the tunnel she'd turned to watch the passengers in the train and seen ... herself. For a second, she thought she might be mistaken, but the girl in the train was staring back at her as amazed as she was herself. They were twins, so much alike in every way. Emmy's jaw dropped and she returned the stare with equal astonishment.

If there was any difference at all, it was in the eyes. Emmy saw straight away that the girl in the train knew things. Emmy knew nothing, neither how to read nor how to write and certainly not how to grow up. She saw straight away, even at that distance, even in those few moments, that the girl in the train understood all this and more. Emmy felt as if she was looking into a whole different world, where love unrolled a magic flying carpet on which you could see and know all there was to see and know.

She waved. It was just an instinct, a hope. It was contact.

The girl in the train waved back and Emmy's heart leapt!

When the train had passed, Emmy stared after it, wondering if the vision had been a dream. She stood stone still, scared to move and lose the moment and the feeling.

And what was that feeling? She wasn't sure, except that it was good, and good feelings were rare enough.

Emmy scrambled down the bank into the tunnel, sat on the stone parapet and hugged herself, rocking backwards and forwards as if praying. The face she had seen burned in her mind, her own face, but full of light and cleverness and love. Emmy wanted to laugh, to cry, to shout, to think. They'd waved at each other! That meant...well, that meant everything. It meant the girl in the train liked her, liked Emmy!

She sat there until the cold began to seep through the stone into her body, but the light of The Girl's face warmed her and gave her hope. She wasn't sure of what, but that didn't matter, hope was good. She didn't know what would happen, whether they would see each other again, whether they might, somehow, in some way...meet, actually meet, and talk! Emmy looked up, her eyes watering, because here was the chance of a friend, not just any friend, but someone special. She just knew it. Something had to happen!

She climbed up the bank and raced home, faster than she'd ever run, swift as a hare. Who was this twin on the train, where did she live, where was she going and what was she like? So many questions!

One more, then. What was her name?

She considered a hundred different names. It shouldn't have been important, a name was just a name, yet somehow it made all the difference.

Was she proud, gentle, kind, cruel, friendly, hurtful, funny, serious? All these things could be changed with a name. A name would pin her down, make her real and solid. There were hard names and soft names floating in the air, and Emmy tried picking them out and sticking them onto The Girl.

Every name had its good and bad points but the one she liked best would be similar to her own, not exactly the same, but close.

She murmured her own name over and over, trying to think of one that sounded right, 'Emmy, Emmy, Emmy, Em ....'

3   Emma Chandler

Emma pushed hard, her arms motoring, her legs pounding the race track. Next day there was a meeting with Maybury School and this was Emma's last chance to practise. Her teachers told her she was good and she knew she was good, top in class, first on the track. She loved the excitement of running, never tired, and was the golden girl in one of the best schools in the country. Cal, her brother, might be Head Boy of his school, but one day Emma would be Head Girl of her school. If there was a baby school, Benjy would no doubt have been Head Baby.

"You're slowing!" called Mrs. Sumner, the sports teacher. "Don't let the arms drop, Emma. Watch the leg action, too, nice steady pace."

Emma focused on her style, listening to Mrs. Sumner, trying to keep her back straight, her legs controlled, her arms pumping neatly. It was easy to forget and start wobbling around, losing time, and time was everything.

She trained every day, sprinting and jogging and, because her school was surrounded by beautiful greenery, cross-country. She also worked in the gym, though she was too young to do the heavy stuff some of the Year Tens and Elevens did, but that would come.

Emma didn't just want to do well, she wanted to win. Her parents, as kind and loving as they were, wanted her to win, too. Mrs. Sumner, as good a sports lady as she was, wanted the same thing. They didn't press it, but Emma knew she was their golden girl.

All schools competed, sometimes one against the other, sometimes in larger competitions. Emma hadn't lost a race yet, and she didn't intend to lost against Maybury, even though they had a pretty good team. Mrs. Sumner reassured her that even if she did lose, it was all part of learning, but Emma didn't believe she meant it. Winning was the name of the game.

The secret was concentration. You had to concentrate on every part of your body and focus the mind. If you let your mind or body wander, you would lose. Emma always concentrated on whatever she was doing, not just running, but schoolwork, homework, drama class, riding, ice skating, reading, even watching television. Her mind worked like a laser, straight and true.

That day, though, her mind was not focused.

It had been three months, a long time. She and her mother were on their way to London on one of their Saturday journeys to see Emma's grandparents. She had been looking out of the window across the marshes, imagining running across the endless, open expanse. Race tracks were fine and the country around the school was all very lovely, but there was something about the marshes which was wild and free. It was also close to the marshes that the Olympic Stadium was going to be built, and when she thought of that her heart missed a beat. No one spoke about it because they didn't want to get too excited, but Emma, her parents and Mrs. Sumner, not to mention the entire school, thought she might, she just might, be good enough to compete in the Olympics when they were held in London in 2012. It seemed ages and ages away, but already the word was out about which pupils in which schools were good enough to train for the Olympics, and Emma's name was always mentioned. Emma couldn't help thinking about it, being good enough to race in the Olympic Games in London, racing against the best in the world, and winning. She pictured the crowds and the excitement and the cameras and the glory, and this spurred her on to train harder.

But it wasn't the Olympics that was distracting her, it was The Girl.

They had caught sight of each other at the same moment. It was only a few seconds, but they were seconds which still echoed down the days.

Emma's mother was reading, Benjy was asleep and Emma was looking out of the window. She didn't have time to think. A figure scrambled out from a tunnel beneath the railway line, a girl, her back to the train. The girl turned and, purely by chance, caught Emma's eye.

They stared in amazement.

Emma was looking at a mirror image of herself, perhaps smaller and frailer, but an incredible likeness. The girl was as astonished as Emma, and their eyes locked in a fleeting moment of recognition and wonder. Unexpectedly, the girl on the marshes lifted a hand and waved, hesitantly, as if she weren't at all sure what response she would get. Without thinking, Emma waved back, just as uncertainly, just for a second. As the train sped on, Emma stretched her neck to look and saw the girl still standing, still as stone, in the distance.

When she sat back, she thought her heart might break from looking at the little lost waif. She felt something inside her change.

Until then, she had been happy in her world, with everything she needed and no reason for

15

uncertainty. But when she saw this other self, something touched her, and each day the magic of that touch deepened, forcing her to question things that she never in a million years thought she would question.

Three months on and, after more stares and waves, she was still questioning.

"Penny for your thoughts, Emma," said Mrs. Sumner as Emma relaxed after four laps of the track.

"Nothing," said Emma. "Just thinking about Maybury."

"Maybury will come and go," said Mrs. Sumner, "you have to focus on your performance."

Her parents told her the same thing. "Life is like a race track," said her father, "only you never stop. You keep going and you do your best, even if others overtake you, and they will, one day," although no one had overtaken Emma on the racetrack yet. "Make the best of all your gifts," said her mother, "win or lose."

When she raced, she raced to win; when she rode her horse, she aimed to be the best rider; when she studied, she wanted to be the cleverest. All the girls in the school were taught to aim high, but they couldn't all get to the finishing line first. Even Emma had to put up with second place sometimes, though never when it came to running.

All these pressures made it frustrating for her not to be as focused as she knew she should be. Since that first sighting, she looked for The Girl whenever she travelled to London. It had become the highlight of the journey every Saturday, when she saw her, looking out for Emma as much as Emma looked out for her, but still half-hiding, shyly, ducking under cover when the train passed by.

Emma's heart longed to reach out and touch her, she seemed so poor, so lost, so everything that Emma wasn't, and though she tried to put such thoughts out of her mind for the competition with Maybury, she couldn't. Emma tried to picture the girl's family, her school, her friends, and it all appeared so very different to her own.

She never spoke to anyone about the girl on the marshes. Her friends and family, would only laugh and think she was being stupid; besides, it was a private and secret friendship with a meaning she had to discover for herself.

Everything was laid on for them when they arrived at Maybury School the next day. They were treated like royalty, given plush changing rooms, visited by the Head Teacher, asked if they needed anything and told they would be offered a mini-banquet after the competition.

Emma was going to run in the fifteen hundred metres, four laps of the track. She was up against Jessica Willard, a girl with a reputation as good as her own, and Emma was keen to see how good Jessica was. Usually, Emma led from the front, but that was because no one could keep up with her. Jessica was a different class. Emma followed her, staring at her golden hair, tied in a pigtail, bouncing around, and was surprised at her own thoughts. She didn't seem to care what happened and all her ambition to race at the Olympics faded. Nothing seemed to matter.

Except one thing.

Emma wondered how someone you'd never met, would never meet, had only seen for seconds, at a distance, could suddenly be so important and everything else fade away, even running, which was such a big part of her life. The Girl's sad, beseeching eyes haunted her, every day, every moment, as if there was an important message there which couldn't and shouldn't be ignored. She saw those eyes now, in the race with Jessica Willard, longing for something just out of reach.

Click.

Emma saw Jessica Willard stretching away in front and snapped out of her reverie.

She switched into gear.

Starting the final lap, she was still a way behind. She couldn't remember the first three. She had been deep in thought. All those lessons about timing and pacing went out the window. She'd been in another world and that wouldn't do. She wasn't out of breath, and though Jessica was fast, she was tiring because she'd been leading the whole time and anxious that Emma was going to catch her.

And Emma did.

She caught up and overtook Jessica who glanced sideways with a look of desperation. There were cheers and gasps as Emma eased into the lead and kept the lead, around the final bend and down the home straight to the finishing tape.

She found Mrs. Sumner there, beaming.

"Emma! Amazing! Wonderful! Words fail me!"

Even the Maybury sports teacher congratulated Emma.

"Can't get you to swap schools, could I?" he asked.

Emma turned to Jessica who looked exhausted.

"Good race," Emma said.

Jessica looked up, her face red.

"I need to train harder," she said. "You're really great."

Emma was pleased she had won, of course, but she felt sorry for Jessica. She must have had so much pressure on her to win, and she hadn't won. That was the trouble with winning, Emma thought, a thought which hadn't bothered her much before, for every winner there were countless losers. Jessica had that terrible, heartrending beaten look.

Emma's parents were delighted.

"Darling, you're a star!" said her mother.

"Our golden girl!" said her father, squeezing Emma's shoulder.

"Just lucky," said Cal, ruffling his sister's hair.

Benjy just laughed.

Emma went to bed that night, her mind echoing with praises. But there were other echoes, too. She had won a race, that was all. What was so different this time? This time it didn't matter as much because something far more important was happening. Without any evidence at all, Emma knew The Girl was unhappy. Emma was the lucky one of the two, imagining some balance of happiness and unhappiness in their lives. But even if this was all fancy, how could Emma feel delight at simply winning a race when her unknown friend might be alone and miserable?

Her head and heart were full, not of the excitement of winning against Jessica Willard, but of the mysterious figure on the marshes who had come to mean so much to her, a figure so wrapped in mystery that, if she didn't know better, Emma might say she'd seen a …

4   Train Ghost

'**G**host!'
Emma tried not to think the word, but she couldn't help herself. 'This is a ghost,' was what she thought, 'and I'm alone with it on a deserted train.'

It was all she could do not to run, scream or just bury her head in her hands and hope the nightmare might vanish.

"Who are you?" she asked, her voice dry and fearful.

The whispering stopped and the ghost seemed to search out Emma. It didn't speak, just moved its head, looking with unseen eyes.

"Say something," said Emma, unwilling to go closer.

"Say somefing," repeated the ghost. Its voice was quiet, almost timid, not threatening, more questioning, testing the air.

Emma, for all her cleverness, struggled to understand.

"What do you want?" she asked. "What's happening? You're not going to hurt me are you?"

The ghost raised its head and replied,

"Need 'elp."

"You need help?"

"No," the ghost replied. "You need 'elp."

Emma caught her breath for a moment.

"To get me out of here?"

The ghost nodded.

"You ain't alone," it said. "Don't wanna be alone 'ere. No good."

It was true, wherever Emma was, whatever had happened, here was something, no matter how weird, to speak with. Company.

"But you gotta do somefing," the ghost went on. "S'important."

"What?" Emma asked.

She watched as the ghost floated off towards the junction of two carriages.

Set up high in the wall was a recessed area in which there was a large, red button.

The emergency stop button.

"Gotta stop the train." the ghost said.

Emma followed, but didn't feel that sturdy on her legs and had to hold on to the seat backs to regain her balance. Her head started throbbing and when she moved she didn't feel comfortable. The ghost watched her.

"You ain't so good, are you?"

"Not really. Don't know what the matter is. I want to go home."

"You will," the ghost said in a voice, anxious but encouraging. "You gotta do this though. I can't do it for you. I would if I could, but I can't."

Emma shook her head. She read the notice below the button.

"I can't either," she said. "Read it. It's illegal. I'm not allowed."

The ghost looked at the writing but said nothing.

"I can't read too good," the ghost admitted. "Woz it say?"

Perhaps the ghost came from the past, Emma

thought, when children didn't go to school. Emma pointed to each word.

"*'Emergency stop. Penalty for improper use.'*"

"There," said Emma. "That's why I can't do it."

The ghost stared at the words and repeated them.

"*'Emergency stop. Penalty for improper use.'*"

"Fanks. Woz it mean?"

Emma blinked.

"It means whoever presses it and stops the train has to have a good reason or else there's a penalty."

"A wot?"

"A penalty. A punishment."

The ghost thought for a moment.

"No one's gonna punish you," it said.

"No. I told you. I'm not going to."

The ghost paused.

"They can't do nuffing to you," it said. "It ain't wrong to press it. Not now."

"Tell me why, then," Emma said. "And I'll do it."

The ghost wouldn't, or couldn't. All it said was,

"Becoz you gotta trust me. Thas why I'm 'ere. Iss serious an' real, y'know. It ain't a dream."

Confusion and panic. Emma breathed deeply, taking in what the ghost had said, what it wanted her to do and still hoping she was going to wake with everything back to normal. This couldn't be real! Nothing she had ever learned or believed could explain it. Her head hurt and she realised she was forgetting things. Memories were muddled. She even had the idea that she ought to know this ghost, and was digging in her memory to see if it really was someone in her life, but she saw little more than what lay beyond the train windows - nothing.

A chill passed through Emma's body and she trembled. The ghost stopped still, and asked,

"Are you cold?"

"I'm okay, but thank you for asking."

She went into the main carriage to rest a moment, tired and sleepy. Bits of her hurt, her mind was shaken and the ghost, who was there supposedly to help, wanted her to do something wrong and dangerous. She felt like giving up, it was all too lonely and terrible for words, ghost or no ghost. She stared out of the window, despondent.

"Might help to think of somefing," the ghost said, gently. "Or someone."

It pointed towards the window and Emma saw a face appear, golden hair falling down a pretty face that belonged to a girl, about Emma's age, laughing and joking in uncanny silence with what must have been imaginary people, because there was no one around her. Emma whispered, excitedly,

"I know her!"

The girl didn't hear, didn't see, didn't respond at all.

"Whass 'er name?" asked the ghost.

"I do know her. I remember her. She's..."

Emma dug deep but the name wouldn't come.

"Jessica ... " prompted the ghost.

Emma turned.

"Willard!" she exclaimed. "I was just going to say it was her! I raced against her!" Then she stared at the ghost. "How did you know?"

"You told me," it answered.

"I didn't! I never did. We've only just met!"

23

Emma didn't wait for the ghost to answer but called to Jessica.

"Jessica! Jessica Willard! Look at me! Can't you see me?"

Jessica couldn't see Emma, but neither could Emma see the people Jessica was talking to. Nevertheless, she was talking still, and laughing and sharing secrets.

"We raced together," Emma said, "and I won! Don't you remember? Jessica! Jessica!"

Emma tried to touch Jessica's face, but all she touched was the cold pane of glass.

"Are you doing this?" she asked the ghost, angrily.

"I ain't doin' nuffing," said the ghost. "Wish I could, though. You gotta do it all."

Emma despaired of understanding. She turned to the vision in the window and tried to remember the race. She definitely ran against her at some school or other ... Merry ... Marry ... Mary ... oh ...! Names kept escaping her. What was the matter? And how come the ghost knew it and she didn't?

Her parents always taught her that problems could be solved with the mind and not with muscle. You could shout and scream and hit out, but in the end you wouldn't solve anything. You had to use your brain. Emma wanted to, but she was confused because too many things were happening that shouldn't be happening. It was impossible to think logically when there was nothing logical to think about.

Jessica was still there, laughing silently with her invisible friends. It was like looking at television with the sound turned down and the box taken away. Emma listened, thinking she might be able to hear what Jessica was saying, but there was nothing to hear.

And then, even as Emma looked, Jessica was gone and Emma was left staring at the emptiness beyond the window.

She closed her eyes.

"Tell me her name," Emma asked, without thinking.

"Jessica Willard," whispered the ghost, reluctantly, as if its words would hurt Emma, and they did.

"I forgot again," Emma said, forlornly, and she collapsed on to a seat, covered her face and cried. The ghost hovered around her, then floated away.

Emma wiped her eyes and looked around to see where the ghost had gone, hoping she hadn't frightened it away – better the company of the ghost than utter loneliness. It hadn't vanished - it was looking down on her and Emma felt its concern. She didn't know how, but sensed the ghost meant her no harm.

"I thought you'd gone," Emma said.

The ghost came closer to Emma and whispered,

"I wouldn't leave you Emma Chandler. I'll never…."

5   Emmy's World

"Go," said Emmy's father, "upstairs or outside if you want. Me and my friends have got to talk, Em. Business stuff."

He gestured to two men sitting at the table. Emmy glanced at them, a glance that sent shivers down her spine – something about the way they looked at her.

"I'll go out," she said.

"Emmy ..." her father started to ask something. She turned to him, but he hesitated and just said, mysteriously, "Sometimes you have to do things you don't want to do. That's life."

She wasn't sure if he meant himself or her, but she guessed he was going to get mixed up in something stupid again. She could worry about that later. For the moment, he didn't want her around, so as it was still light out, she headed for the marshes.

She crossed to the new developments full of tidy bungalows with bright cherry red roofs and neat gardens, then over the footbridge onto the edge of the wilder areas where she sat on a bench throwing pebbles into the canal. The canal wasn't that wide here, but it was deep, and stretched for miles both north and south. She'd once run the south bit until she got almost to the River Thames, but she'd never run north, at least not that far. The canal was part of an old network of waterways linking the whole country. Emmy imagined herself, one day when she'd had enough of her father, leaving home, school and everything and just running forever, seeing what went on in the world.

People cycled as well as walked along the old tow path, when it was clear and wide enough, and sometimes even when it wasn't clear and wide enough. Wandering off the beaten track, it became hard at times to tell you were in London, the landscape was grass and scrubland, water and sky; it was only in the distance you could see evidence of cities and of humanity carving up the world.

The pebbles plopped into the water one after the other. Emmy aimed them, in her imagination, at her father, throwing them a little harder. She wondered if she had two hearts, one for hating, one for loving, because that was what it felt like. She couldn't see how the same heart loved so much and hated so much.

He'd read her a story once. Just the once. It must have been a good day. She remembered him laughing and joking around and then, when she went to bed, saying he'd read to her. She was six and he'd never read a story to her in her little life. Even now she didn't know what had made him do it, but he had, and it was special. Other fathers probably read to their children every night, but Emmy had to make the most of the single occasion and remember it forever.

She remembered it then, and threw an extra large stone in frustration. Whenever she felt the anger build inside her, she ran. Running filled her with joy. It didn't matter that she had no kit. She saw people jogging along, all geared up, but most had no style and Emmy would overtake them, effortlessly, an inner fury driving her on. It might have been fun to have some fancy trainers and a bright track suit, but she would never have them and didn't miss them.

She stood up, looked around, planned a route,

and set off.

Although they were called marshes, they weren't particularly marshy. There was a different feel wherever you went. By the old greyhound racetrack it felt spooky because people had been there but left it all to fall apart; by Bomb Crater Pond it was more wild and mysterious; there was the nature reserve which was peaceful, and the open marsh which was busier, and the marina area which was exciting. It wasn't the wisest thing to go alone into the marshes, not at any age, especially when you were twelve years old, going on thirteen, but Emmy wasn't bothered. She couldn't imagine much worse than a bad dad with worse friends. Besides, she knew she could run if she had to, or fight back if push came to shove.

There was nowhere else and nothing else. She didn't fit at school and was unwanted at home. Here, she felt free. Her feet hardly touched the ground as she flew along, breathing in the evening air, imagining as she ran that she was escaping everything and everyone that made her life so unhappy. For those minutes, there was relief. No one could touch her here, and all the nastiness that surrounded her vanished.

She reached the level crossing and paused, not so much for breath, because she was never out of breath, but to think about her friend, The Girl. What she was doing now? Perhaps she was doing homework, because she was clever, or was with a family that loved her to bits. Maybe she was with friends – she must have so many!

Emmy heard a train coming and scrambled down the embankment, under the bridge. As ever, it was dark, damp and solitary. She hoped no one would come by as the train approached.

You could hear it, louder and louder, but as soon as it was directly overhead the sound changed. You were enveloped by thunder, not just above, but all around, as if the walls of the tunnel magnified and concentrated the noise and made your whole body vibrate. Emmy screamed, releasing the fury.

Instantaneously, the sound stopped and the rumblings faded. Emmy knew exactly when the final carriage had passed over the level crossing. She climbed up and saw the train disappearing northwards towards Cambridge. How she wished she was on it! She'd never been on a train. Maybe one day she would do it and The Girl would be there in Cambridge to greet her.

Reluctantly, she set off home, taking a long route along the far end of the marshes towards the Lea Bridge Road. She didn't stop to look a the traffic, an endless line of almost stationary cars from way back to way ahead. She stayed by the river and crossed under the road, heading into the old waterworks. This had a little atmosphere of its own, too, with broken bricks and great tumbling stones from the ancient pumping station. It was hard to run there, but she kept going, fleet as a mountain goat. One or two people were about, walking their dogs or just walking with each other, but it was quiet and peaceful and Emmy loved it.

She wasn't sure whether to get back sooner or later. It was difficult with dad. She rarely got things right with him. She had a feeling that tonight she better not get back too early, so she ran on, almost up to the old matchbox factory where she paused, looked at its grim brick walls and broken windows, then turned back.

A barge drifted along the river and the old man

who was steering it watched Emmy jogging along the river bank.

"Careful you don't fall in, lovey," he called.

Sometimes, the shrubs growing by the edge of the Lea Navigation were overgrown, and Emmy had to fight her way through tangles of branches and spiky leaves, but she ducked and dived and wove her way through to clearer patches, just as she tried to fight her way through all the difficult and wrong people in her life.

Home was the least clear patch of all.

Dad was sitting in the living room with the same two men, Saul, a tall, rangy, spectral man, and Victor, heavy set, rock-like.

All three looked at her as she came in as if they'd just been talking about her.

Victor, who smiled like splitting rock, said, "Welcome home, sweetheart. How about a cup of tea for your dad and his friends?"

Emmy bridled at being given orders by a stranger in her own home, but her father nodded, so she turned into the kitchen without a word, wishing the men would leave.

They didn't.

Bits of conversation floated in, enough for her to get a depressing picture of what they were discussing. She didn't know why her dad kept such company. They were no good - and neither, she feared, was he.

She put the teas and biscuits on a tray and took them in to the three men.

"Don't suppose you heard anything, did you Em?" asked Victor.

Saul, quietly attentive, listened to her answer. He

listened to everything.

"No. Course not."

"What would you do if you ever did hear anything, Em?" Victor asked.

"She wouldn't do anything," Emmy's dad answered for her. "She knows where her bread's buttered. Isn't that right Emmy?"

Emmy nodded and was going to leave, when Victor called her back.

"Emmy," he said, "how do you feel about a bit of an adventure?"

She'd been afraid of this. Her heart began to beat a little faster.

They waited for her answer.

Emmy's father didn't come to her rescue. He just sat land stared at the floor, too weak to act.

"Dunno," Emmy replied.

"Dunno!" Victor echoed. "What kind of answer is that, Emmy? You're a bright girl, aren't you?"

"No," she replied.

"Well just suppose," Victor went on. "Wouldn't you like to earn a bit of extra cash?"

Emmy saw she'd never be allowed to leave the room unless she gave an answer, but she really didn't know what to say. 'No' wasn't an option.

"Suppose."

Victor and Saul looked at each other. Emmy's father looked up at his daughter.

"Is that a yes or a no?" Victor asked.

"Dunno," Emmy replied. "Wot've I gotta do?"

She knew immediately that she should have said no, but Victor and Saul scared her and the damage was done. She'd shown interest. Victor put a hand on her

31

shoulder and squeezed it.

"Don't worry, Em," he said, "you never know. Maybe we won't need you. Don't mind us asking, do you?"

Emmy squirmed away. Victor was strong as an ox. Emmy hated his touch.

"Leave her be," said her father.

Emmy looked at her father blankly, without thanks. It was his fault these brutes were in their house.

Victor laughed and let her go. She breathed out and left them, relieved.

Later that night, when the two men were gone, Emmy's father came to her room.

"Didn't bother you, did they, asking questions?"

"No."

"I mean there's nothing to be afraid of. They're my friends."

Emmy shivered. With friends like that, who needed enemies?

"I don't like 'em. Why do you have to let 'em in our 'ouse?"

William Fairchild had been calm and quiet a moment before, almost friendly, but he turned, as he often did. He went red with anger and fumed,

"Not your business, Emmy, who my friends are. You keep your mouth shut about them. You hear?"

She heard. She wasn't going to say anything anyway. There wasn't anyone to talk to about them, was there?

"You shouldn't have got back early," her father said, sullenly.

"I didn't. Anyway, you threw me out."

Her father scowled at her, as if he resented every

word she said.

"You got back early!" he whispered, emphasising every word.

Emmy didn't know why she said what she did, but she said it anyway. It was the way the peace and freedom of the marshes stacked up against this unhappiness at home.

"I didn't! I got back the time you told me. I always listen! I always do wot you want!"

Her father lifted his hand as if he were going to strike her.

"Go on then!" Emmy taunted him. "Hit me! You bully!"

He hesitated, then lowered his hand.

"Sorry," he whispered. "I just don't want you talking back to me, or to Vic and Saul, especially to them."

Emmy snapped at him.

"You juss don't want me, do you? You're a rubbish dad!"

He looked at her blankly, wanting to make up, but not knowing how.

"I don't want that, silly girl."

"Silly girl! Silly girl!" Emmy repeated, mocking herself as well as her father. She was furious with him.

"I bet her dad's better than you," she said, spitting the words at him. "I bet he doesn't hit his daughter!"

Her father looked at her, puzzled.

"Who you talking about? Whose father?"

Emmy covered her secret.

"Anyone's! They're all better'n you. I hate you!"

She buried her face in her hands and cried until

she heard the door close and her father leave. They might look the same, The Girl on the train and Emmy, but Emmy doubted she had to put up with this. There couldn't be a worse father in the whole nasty, awful, rotten, spiteful...

6   Emma's World

"**W**onderful, amazing world,"
said Emma's father,
pointing at the image
projected on the screen. He was coming to the end of a
talk given to Emma's school. Being a local boffin, the
head teacher had invited him to speak there, and though
he'd been nervous, the talk had gone well. Emma had
been more nervous than her father, afraid the school
would get restless and things might get embarrassing,
but it wasn't that kind of school and everyone seemed to
be listening.

Mr. Chandler worked at a famous observatory
and had spoken about his job there. He was a good
speaker, made lots of jokes and wandered off the subject
quite frequently, which amused everyone. Some children
looked a bit fazed by the whole thing, but most were
fascinated, especially by the photographs projected onto
the screen – dozens of them, amazing pictures which
fired the imagination.

"This is our home and we think this is all there
is," said Mr. Chandler, "but it isn't. There's so much
more. We just don't see it. Ah well. You see, my job
isn't just staring at the universe, it's to unlock its secrets.
Sometimes I feel I'm a traveller on a train hurtling along
and I can't get off - the years whiz by and there's no
time to look and understand the whole mind-boggling
mystery.

"I'm almost done now. One last thing. Think of
all the things that are bothering you right now. Boys?

Girls? Exams? Of course these things bother us, because they're important, but I'll tell you something. You see, I look at the way the universe is made, and the more I see of it, the more I know I will never know. As a scientist, I have to have a clear head to decide what's true and what's not true. You need the same to sort out your problems. How do we do that?"

Silence.

"We look and we think, very hard, very far and very deep. And even then, we can't know it all, and we have to keep an open mind about what might and what might not be possible.

"As you grow up, you'll get some things you want, you won't get others, but there may be only one thing that you want so much, you'll move a mountain for it, because if you don't you'll be unhappy forever, and forever is a long time. Right now, you probably feel that you could do anything, and you're right, you probably could. As you grow older people will tell you that you can't, but it's up to you. I think - and this is what my talk is all about - the world, the galaxy, the universe, is intelligence, not just nice colourful stars, but thought and imagination. I'm not talking about God, that's for someone else to come and tell you about. I'm talking about you, each of you, being magicians. I don't think this universe of ours knows many limits, and I doubt there are any limits at all to what we can imagine and what we can do."

At the end, there was loud applause and lots of questions. Emma was sitting next to Kevin, a classmate, friend and self proclaimed space anorak. He wanted to ask a hundred questions and Emma was relieved her father could answer all the ones Kevin was allowed to

36

ask. But she had questions of her own, only she daren't ask them there, in the hall. She daren't even ask them at all, in case her father, who was frighteningly clever, asked some himself of her, and she wasn't ready to talk yet.

On the way home, he said to her,

"Was I alright?"

"Not bad," she answered.

"I wasn't boring?"

"Just a bit."

"Oh."

"Dad! I was joking. You were great."

"Was I really? I was ever so nervous."

She poked his arm and he laughed.

One sentence in particular, the one about the train, stuck in her mind. That's what she felt like when she was on the real train, seeing her twin that wasn't a twin, wondering who she was, what she was like and what she wanted. She put a scientific twist on it. Perhaps the train passed through some kind of door in a parallel world and there was another Emma Chandler. What would happen if they met? She risked asking her father if it was possible, if doors might open between worlds and you could meet a copy of yourself.

"Doppelgangers," he explained, "Another you." He thought for a moment. "I don't think they could ever meet. It would break all the laws of physics."

She plied Kevin at school with questions and he was surprised; he didn't think a girl could be interested in such things. He even thought she might be interested in him, but she wasn't; she simply wanted to understand why this vision from the train had affected her so much.

She did some research on the net, but it was hard

to tell fact from fiction. She was impatient to see the girl again, to judge for herself what might be happening.

The following Saturday, there she was. Emma's mother was sleeping and Benjy was also dozing, but Emma was wide awake, watching intently as the girl ducked and dived, staring one moment, hiding the next, half child, half adult. Emma tried to imagine she was looking into a different universe, that the train was passing through some hole in space and time, but it didn't feel true. The girl watched her with Earthly eyes and Emma looked back with Earthly eyes. They were girls from two different paths in life who happened to resemble each other and who desperately wanted to meet.

The mystery lay elsewhere, in something very human, but it was no less interesting. And Emma did indeed feel that there were new worlds involved, only not ones you could see with a telescope, but ones inside her head.

"You look a bit preoccupied, Emma," said her father one evening, "Still bathing in the glow of my fame are you?"

"Ha ha."

"Anything bothering you?"

"No," she answered, too quickly

"You can always talk to me, or mum, whenever you want. You know that, don't you?"

There were things she wanted to ask, but couldn't. She took refuge in her books and in her running. She was only free when she ran and her mind cleared when she pounded the track or the leaf strewn woods on a cross country. She felt so much energy flowing through her, as if she could, like her father had

38

said, take on the world and do anything she wanted. She wanted to do so much, to learn everything there was to learn, to run faster than the wind, to understand life. She was growing up and a zillion thoughts raced through her mind faster than she could race along any track.

Teachers commented that she wasn't as single minded as she'd been. They asked her if she was alright and if something was troubling her. This was scary. She feared that adults could read her thoughts, that nothing was secret. Even her friends told her she was acting weird, although she tried to keep things going as normal. And they were normal. There was no big deal about what had happened, it was just a coincidence and if she told people, then it wouldn't be affect her so much any more.

But something inside her said she should keep quiet about it, and she did, telling no one. Nevertheless, she needed to do something, and a plan began to form, but she was so shocked by it that she tried to put it out of her head straight away. It wouldn't budge, though. Like a lot of thoughts that had suddenly come into her head, she seemed to have no control over it, and Emma didn't like losing control.

During a science class at school she absent-mindedly picked up a prism and looked through it at her friends and the rest of the class. That's what she saw when she looked at her world now, something distant and mysterious, even distorted; it was only clear when she looked out of the train window.

"What are you doing, Emma?" one of the girls asked.

She tried to get back on track, but it didn't matter what she did, she was always distracted. Her friends were going out more and more, but she went out with them less and less, and even when she did go, her mind was elsewhere. The secret she was keeping dominated everything else. She believed there was something so important to be discovered that it would change her life, but that if she told anyone, the whole thing would fall apart and nothing would happen at all.

Not that things were bad and needed changing, they weren't and they didn't. It was just intuition, a strong feeling that here was something more important than anything else, than schoolwork, music, riding, even than running.

The only one she felt comfortable with during these days was Benjy. Benjamin Chandler was her biggest fan and needed her more than anyone else, just as she needed him. She would read to him at night, feed him when mum was busy, play with him when he had no friends around, talk to him when he wanted to listen, and listen when he wanted to talk.

"Emma upset," he said one night.

"No I'm not."

"Yes. Are."

"No. Not."

"Y…"

She tickled him to stop him contradicting her and he laughed out loud.

"I'll read you a story, Benjy," she said.

He went quiet and listened, laying on his bed with eyes full of adoration. Emma brushed his hair back and read him The Match Girl. He hung on every word.

"You Match Girl," he said, when she'd finished.

Emma looked surprised.

"Why did you say that?"

"Because you are."

"I don't sell matches."

"Yes you do."

"And I'm not poor."

"Yes you are."

"Right. And I suppose I'm cold and hungry."

"Yes you are."

Emma looked at her brother and wondered what went on in his tiny head. He could make up anything about anything – it was only what he wanted. Oddly, she felt as if she was doing the same thing, in a more grown up way, but still making up her own world with its own rules, and she was ignoring what was really happening.

And what was this?

She'd become obsessed with something that was just chance. It meant only what she wanted it to mean, and it probably meant nothing at all. She was becoming edgy because of nothing and she determined to deal with it, either by telling someone or…well, it was that idea again, so disturbing she ought not think about it ever again.

She buried her head in her books, ran more and faster than ever, kept as busy as she could and even decided one Saturday not to go to London. Her mother said,

"Mum and dad won't like that Emma. They love to see you."

'Mum and dad' were mum's mum and dad and Emma knew they would miss her, but she was trying to build a distance between her and her secret twin.

It didn't work. She was so anxious the following week, thinking that the girl on the marshes would be worried, or worse, be upset. She might think Emma didn't want to see her any more and that wasn't true. Emma was just trying to do the right thing, but the right thing wasn't easy to recognise.

The Saturday after, she looked out of the train window and the girl was there, the same as ever, with that unspeakably sad, heart-rending look.

"I had a letter from your Head Teacher," her father said at supper one evening. Emma tensed. She thought she might be in trouble, that all this worrying over nothing was affecting her work. But it wasn't that. "He wanted to thank me," Mr. Chandler went on, "for the talk. Thought it was one of the best things the school had done this year and he wants me to do it again next year. There you are, Emma, I'm a hit."

Emma breathed a sigh of relief.

"I told you," she said. "You should be a teacher, dad."

"Not likely. Too much work, not enough money," he answered. "It was fun, though."

Emma's mother then said, "I have news, too."

Immediately, Emma became anxious again. This was crazy. But the news was nothing to do with her.

"I've got a commission," she said. "Look."

She passed round a letter and they read it in turn. Emma's mother still managed to keep her work going, and here she was with a real live commission from the BBC to make a green documentary for television.

"Mum!" said Calum. "You'll be famous!"

"Not really, Cal, but I'm delighted. You know I'm into green."

Looking around at her family, Emma knew she was lucky and that she'd better sort her head out quickly or she could mess everything up. She didn't know how, but she knew for certain that if she kept this secret to herself and did anything like what she was planning to do, it would be a disaster, perhaps even a bigger one than she could imagine. Her mum and dad were in the best of moods. Calum had come back victorious from a rugby match. Even Benjy banged the table with his spoon in delight, though he had no idea what was happening.

This was the time to say something. They were all together, they were in a good mood, they would support her and understand her, she knew it. All she had to say was this, 'Mum, dad, I want to tell you something. When we go to London on a Saturday, I see this girl hiding on the marshes. I know it sounds weird, but she looks just like my twin sister and I can't stop thinking about her. I think she's in trouble and needs my help. I don't know how I know, but I do. If I don't help her, no one will, and there's some kind of connection there. It's bothering me. I can't concentrate on school and I even think about her when I'm running. She's my doppelganger, dad, that thing you told me about? I don't know what to do, but I want to do something. There. I've told you.'

It really would be an easy thing to say, and she knew it would be a weight off her mind. But at the same time, she knew what they would say. 'Darling, you have a heart of gold, but there are some things where we just can't interfere. You can point her out to us on the train and we'll see for ourselves, but I doubt we can do anything. There are lots of people out there who might look a bit like us, but we can't go chasing after them, it isn't sensible. She's probably fine, this girl, and you know Emma, sometimes you can think you're doing the right thing and you're not, you're doing the wrong thing. The way to destruction is paved with good intentions. Haven't you heard that? It's true.'

They would say something like this. Emma heard the whole conversation in her head. Then she'd be stuck. They'd watch her, keep an eye on her, and maybe do something to get the girl in trouble, like telling the police. Emma didn't want that. As good as her life was, she had nothing in it that was private, and this needed to be private. Her mum and dad couldn't feel what she felt, the same compassion, understanding, sympathy and interest. They weren't just similar, she and the girl, they were identical, freakily identical.

The moment passed. They talked of other things and Emma knew she wasn't going to say anything, not there, not then.

And now Benjy was causing a commotion. He was playing with one of his toys, a little pink elephant of all things, trying to get it to speak. There was a button on it and he was pulling it for all it was worth.

"Benjy baby," said dad, "if you want to be a boffin like good old daddy, you have to look at things to see how they work. No good just pulling everything to bits. See, read that. Can you read?"

"Yes."

"Fibber. And you four years old. It doesn't say pull it, Benjy, it says ... "

7   Train Ghost

"Push it," said the ghost, quietly, "it'll stop the train. You 'ave to stop it soon, y'know."

Emma believed this now, but she couldn't explain it and she couldn't get herself to do as the ghost asked, not yet.

"Can't," she replied. "Sorry."

"S'alright," the ghost answered. "I fink you trust me a bit. Thas good. How you feelin'?"

Emma wasn't feeling brilliant, but it was comforting having the ghost ask. She would have been desperate all alone in the deserted train. The ghost knew that and was doing what it could to help.

Emma had been gazing into the window where she had seen Jessica, such a long time ago, it seemed. She wanted to see her again, or to see some memory of the life that was rapidly fading, but she had seen nothing. The ghost gently raised its wispy tendrils of a hand, pointed and ever so slowly, drifting into view like a phantom, a boy's face appeared. Emma watched, unafraid, even a little excited.

"You see him?" Emma asked. "I know him, but…"

She tried so hard to remember. The silence in the train, as eerie as it had been, was even more eerie with this strange threesome, a girl, a ghost, a vision.

Bells in Emma's head. A talk. A school. A friend.

"Kevin," she said to the ghost, after minutes, or was it hours, of searching. "His name was Kevin. There was a talk...my father was talking, at school, telling us things, clever things...."

"Go on," the ghost encouraged her.

Emma tried, but it was so hard, and she felt extraordinarily tired. The image of Kevin floated in the world beyond the window and Emma touched the glass to make some kind of contact, but as soon as she did, the vision vanished. She sat back, tears in her eyes. The ghost reached out to her as Emma had reached out to Kevin, but Emma felt only the tiniest hint of a gentle breeze. She flinched.

"We gotta work togever, not be afraid of each uvver," said the ghost, softly, "Thas the only way. Iss like your memory's tryin' to tell you fings," it went on. "Somefing to do wiv why you're here ... why we're here. Fink back a bit, to before you met me. Where was you?"

Emma moved the broken pieces of her memory, like piecing together a jigsaw. She'd thought she was on the train from Cambridge to London, but she saw other things, too.

"Grass ... a bridge. ...and a shadow of something ... but it's gone."

The ghost listened intently, hanging on to Emma's every word. Emma became aware of how close and attentively the ghost was listening.

"Tell me!" Emma said. "You know something important, don't you? The grass, the bridge, the train, they mean something to you, don't they? I know they do."

The ghost remained quiet, bobbing up and down slightly. It had no form, no definite shape, but Emma could tell how it was feeling and even a little of what it was thinking. She didn't know how she was doing this, but it was undeniable, and what she felt most of all was that the ghost was on her side, wanting to help. It had done nothing since they'd met to hurt or frighten her, and all it wanted was for Emma to remember, and Emma was trying, but she was scared of remembering because there was pain and hurt there. Even so, she wanted to be brave, and this might mean trying to find whatever it was that had somehow become lost and confused.

She felt a bond to this insubstantial thing beside her. She wanted to comfort it as much as it wanted to comfort her. There was something touching and sad about it, something it needed and had never had.

Emma looked at the red button and wondered. Supposing … just supposing … she did it. What would be the worst that could happen? The worst was that she'd be stuck there forever. But the best was that this nightmare would end and she'd back at home with her family.

She tried to stand, but felt wobbly. The ghost wanted to help but couldn't touch or do anything. It was simply there, offering comfort. Whatever it said, whatever it did, it did so with all its attention, all its energy, ever so lovingly. ever so …

8   Emmy At Home

Carefully, Emmy cut the card into a large square. She stared at it for a while as if trying to visualize how the letters and words should look. She practised on some scraps of paper. She held her pen as if it were a hammer, something heavy and cumbersome, not a delicate, intricate tool. She experimented with letter shapes and formed words, wishing she knew someone who could check the spelling, someone she could trust. But she didn't. She would just have to hope the writing made sense. She tried to match the words she'd written with words from books, but it was like looking into a kaleidoscope of confusing patterns.

She'd had the idea a few weeks back. She was twelve, not five or six, and it was shameful not to be able to read and write. She was sure The Girl could write long words and spell them all correctly, that she could read them back and do everything. But she would do her best and you couldn't do more than that. Even if The Girl didn't see it or couldn't read it, at least Emmy was doing something.

She looked at the cut card and stared at the thick black pen, afraid to mark the pure whiteness of the card with her scrawly, scribbly, unreadable words. But she'd been practising for days and so, getting comfortable and balanced, she wrote :

stop and tork to me

When it was done, Emmy inspected it. She supposed it was wrong, but she didn't know how to make it right, so she just hoped it was clear enough to read. The letters were big so that they could be seen a fair distance away, but still she would have to get closer to the train than ever before. If The Girl saw it, she would know it was for her; others might see it, too, but Emmy hoped they wouldn't all get off the train and come and talk to her - that would be a disaster. People who saw it might point and laugh, but that was okay because the laughter might make her twin look, and all Emmy needed was for her to look, to understand and to do it, then everything would be different and better.

That Saturday afternoon she put the card in a plastic bag and was about to leave when her father called her.

"Where you off to, Emmy?"

Emmy tried not to panic. She should have known. Whenever she did anything it went wrong.

"Nowhere," she answered.

This was probably the worst answer she could have given.

"Don't give me nowhere, cheeky monkey. What's in the bag?"

Emmy could have left the house a thousand times with a stupid bag and her father wouldn't have batted an eyelid, but because today she had something important in it he had to stop her. Emmy felt bad luck sticking to her like a shadow.

"School stuff," she said. "I'm gonna do some drawing wiv some friends."

"Since when were you so interested in school stuff?"

49

Emmy didn't answer; least said, soonest mended.

"Well, when you're a famous artist, lend us a few hundred quid," her father joked, then ruffled her hair and let her go.

Emmy turned away and left, not rushing, though she felt like pelting away at top speed, she so dreaded him calling her back. He turned, though, and headed towards the half empty bottle he'd left on the kitchen table.

Emmy jogged off to the level crossing and searched for a good spot to hold up the message, not too close, not too far. It was hard to tell if people in the train would be able to see it clearly, so she tried leaving the card propped up and looking at it from different distances until she felt comfortable that the words were visible.

She waited.

Being a Saturday there were more people than usual, but they tended to wander around the edges of the marshes, not venture into the central area near the train lines and the level crossing. She almost changed her mind. It was such a stupid thing to do and bound not to work. Nobody in their right mind would do this, but Emmy had decided a long time ago that she didn't have a right mind.

A couple of trains passed and Emmy was tempted to try out the message, just to see if people looked, but that would be spoiling it. The message was not just for anyone, it was for someone special.

The train came on time. She saw it in the distance and took the card out from the plastic bag. She checked it, but even if it hadn't been right, there was nothing she could do now.

The train approached and Emmy stared at it, as if she would send a silent message to The Girl to look out of the window. How disappointed Emmy would be if she didn't look, if it was all a big, foolish waste of time!

She stood up straight, waited until the train was thundering past, watching with hawk-like eyes as if nothing else in the world existed. She fixed her gaze on each passing window in case The Girl was in a different place, and she was.

She stood alone by the door, watching.

Emmy couldn't believe it. Good luck!

She lifted the card and held it up in the air, the writing towards the window, hiding shyly behind it. She counted to ten, very slowly, until the train had disappeared, then she lowered the card.

Done.

Or half done.

Six hours later, she did it again, watching the train speed north from London to Cambridge. The Girl was standing by the door again. Emmy lifted the card. This time, she peeped out from behind it, just to see if she was looking. She was, straight at her! And if Emmy didn't know better, she'd say she looked amazed and … perhaps … just perhaps …delighted.

Emmy went home, her spirits miles high, only to see Victor and Saul's car outside. She couldn't take the chance and tore the card into pieces. Victor and Saul weren't as careless as dad. If they saw her with something and were interested, they wouldn't let it pass, and she didn't want them knowing what she'd done. They'd press her and ask questions and it would all be spoiled.

She put the pieces in the dustbin and went inside.

"Emmy!" Victor called out, seeing her try to sneak in without being seen. "Come here dolly girl!"

Emmy went in. The three of them were there, the two villains arrogant and hard, her father sheepish and uncomfortable.

"How are you, Em?" Victor asked.

She hated him being so familiar. She hated him, full stop.

"Alright."

"Just alright? Where you been then?"

"Nowhere."

"You haven't been a bad girl, have you, Emmy?"

"Leave off, Vic," said Mr. Fairchild. "She's a decent enough girl."

Emmy looked at her father. That was the first time she remembered him saying such a thing.

"Course she is!" Victor said. "What do you do out there, on the marshes, Emmy?"

"Nothing. Run."

"Run! What for?"

"I like it. I'm good at it."

"Are you now? So how would you like to do some running for us?"

It was the last thing Emmy wanted to do. The only running she'd do for them would be to run away from them as fast as possible.

"What d'you mean?"

"Come and sit down, Emmy. I'll tell you."

Reluctantly, she sat with them at the table. They'd been having a little talk, Victor said, and they had a plan.

"Your dad doesn't want you involved, Em," said Victor, "but me and Saul, we need you. And we trust you."

Emma was worried. She didn't think they trusted her at all. They just needed her for something rotten, and her dad was too weak to say no.

"You ain't gonna kill anyone?" Emmy asked before she thought what she was asking.

"Only you, if you open your mouth," said Saul.

This was the first time he'd said anything and Emmy hoped it was the last. His voice was rasping and cruel, as if every word was a threat.

"It's a simple enough thing," said Victor, reassuringly. "You'll be able to do it."

Emmy shook her head. She wanted nothing to do with these men, even her weak and bullied father.

"Why not?" asked Victor, pretending surprise.

Emmy didn't answer.

"Leave her out," said Mr. Fairchild. "We can do it without her."

"No," said Victor, "She's got to be in, Will. You'll have to have words with her. She'll do it."

Emmy wished the ground would swallow her up, or better still, swallow Saul and Victor ... and even her dad. She loved him. She hated him. She didn't understand, unless he was as frightened of these two madmen as she was. They would kill her, she felt sure of it. They would kill anyone who didn't do what they wanted. They were big babies that screamed and screamed until they got their way, only these two screamed silently, with looks and invisible messages.

"Tell you what," said Victor, "I'll explain the

details another day. Your dad'll talk to you later, so's you have time to think a little. These things need thinking about, Em. You go off now and we'll talk again soon. Alright?"

She went to her room, wanting to be elated at what she'd done with the message, but Victor had destroyed all the elation. He and Saul were going to ruin everything!

She tried to put them out of her mind, to think about her secret new friend and what might happen, but even as she tried, there was a knock on her door.

It was her father.

"You alright?" he asked.

She nodded.

"Sorry about all that with Victor and Saul," he said.

"I don't wanna do nuffing for them."

"I know. But it isn't a big deal, Emmy. You'd be helping me, too, and helping yourself. Don't look after yourself, who will? But I won't ask my Emmy to do anything she doesn't want to do."

He gave her a fake hug. He was as bad as his friends, worse because he was her father. He would get his own daughter into trouble for money, she knew it. He was so useless!

"You ain't gonna kill no one, are you?" she asked again.

"Kill? No! Course not! I just don't like being poor. I don't like having no money. Nor will you when you grow up. Money's everything in this world, Em. You can be nice as pie but if you ain't got money you're nothing, told you before, tell you again. All them blokes in government, spouting forth this and that, and nothing changes. They wouldn't help the likes of you and me. We have to help ourselves. So do Vic and Saul – I know you don't like them, but they're good at what they do…"

Emmy wondered what that was - murdering people, probably.

"…and it won't be much longer. When the job's done, we won't have to see them any more. Things will be different, you wait and see. I know I'm not always right, but I am on this. We'll have some money, we can go somewhere posh, have a nice holiday, maybe even tell your mum and she'll come back again. Was only me being poor that drove her off. What do you think?"

Emmy didn't know what to think, joy and despair battling it out in her heart and mind.

"Will you do it, then?" asked her father "Just look out for us one night, when we're ready, like. Will you?"

Emmy looked at her father with such a mixture of contempt and love. She wanted to hug him, she wanted to smack him around his stupid, useless face.

But in the end she felt she had no choice and simply said …

9   Emma At Home

"Okay," Emma answered. "I'm coming." Her mother had been calling her for supper, but Emma was locked in her room with her homework and her thoughts. The homework was easy, the thoughts weren't.

She had a hundred good things in her life, but this one mystery dwarfed them all. The quizzical, sad, determined face, the shabby clothes and those eyes shining with a fierce, fighting spirit burned in her memory. She looked around her room, full of everything she needed and wanted. She was so lucky, she knew it, but where was the joy in it all if there was this waif of a girl, so much like her in appearance, who had so little.

"Emma!"

She lay aside the homework, opened the door and went downstairs.

"Must be fascinating homework," said her father.

He'd been proud as punch since the talk and felt closer than ever to his darling daughter.

"What's up, sis?" asked Cal. "You look depressed."

"No, I'm alright. Just thinking."

"Well don't do too much of it, your brain will melt."

They ate together, not just once a week, but whenever possible. They talked about what they'd done during the day and they listened as much as spoke. They rarely argued, just found other ways to solve differences.

If life pulled one of them down, the others would pick them up. A strong bond bound them into a bright, happy family.

"Anything wrong, Emma?" asked her mother.

"No, just busy."

"You do look a bit down," said her father. "A problem shared is a problem spared."

"No, I'm okay."

They didn't press her, but talked away about this and that, which was most subjects under the sun. At twelve, Emma knew what was going on and knew who was making it go on. She had always been the most enthusiastic, the light of their lives, but that evening she couldn't join in, even when challenged, and they always challenged each other, not nastily, just to make the other think harder.

When her father asked about homework, she gave a half-hearted answer and her parents exchanged a concerned look, but they bided their time to see what was bothering their star girl. Once the talking got going, Emma's spirits lifted slightly, but what she really wanted to talk about, she couldn't. It wouldn't make sense. She hadn't even met The Girl, but she thought about her all the time. She wondered whether her mother was like *her* mother, whether her father was like *her* father, whether their homes were similar, but decided that none of these things were the same, that in fact they were unimaginably different.

"You are preoccupied, Emma," said her mother, gently. "Won't you tell us what's bothering you."

Emma felt she had to ask something, but they were such important things, she didn't know how to ask them.

"Why is there unhappiness in the world, then? That's my question."

They all looked at her as if she'd asked the most bizarre question possible, which it might have been; it was certainly unexpected.

"That's the way the world is, Emma," her mother answered. "Things aren't as bad as they used to be, though."

"No," said Cal, "a hundred years ago, you'd be living in a horrid little house with an outside loo, there'd be no heating, no hot water and you'd really be miserable. Why are you asking, Em?"

"Just for school stuff. But ... well ... don't you think it's wrong that lots of people are still poor?"

"Of course it's wrong, dear," her mother answered, "there are lots of wrong things in the world. It isn't a perfect place, you know that. You just have to do the best you can."

"Listen to the news," said Cal, who had become quite confident and even a touch thoughtless by the old age of eighteen, "it's all about what's gone wrong. Every day. Nothing new about being poor or unhappy. You're not joining the Salvation Army or something, are you Emma?"

"Cal!" his mother scolded him. "Emma's only asking what we all ask ourselves. There aren't easy answers, sweetheart. I wish there were. I wish we could wave a magic wand and get rid of all the unfairness, but we can't. Why are you asking, Emma, it isn't just school work, is it?"

"I was just thinking about it."

"Good that you do," said her father, "These are important things and if you don't think about them, they'll never get fixed."

Emma wondered if they would get fixed anyhow. Things didn't get fixed by talking about them, they only got fixed by people doing things. The world was such a busy, busy place, yet no one had busied themselves with The Girl who seemed to live outside of everything normal. Seeing her was like looking through a peephole into somewhere that wasn't shown on the news, talked about at home, or read about in the papers, a clue that something was not working properly.

Emma found it hard to enjoy the things the way she'd enjoyed them before she'd seen her mysterious twin. She couldn't think of much else except finding out about her and helping her. She wanted so much to do something rather than just think about it, and there was only one thing to do.

The idea had started as a tiny seed then grew until it became huge and she bumped into it at every turn.

For weeks she did nothing, just tried to fight the idea because it was too foolish to consider. But one Saturday morning she was on the train to London when, on an impulse, just before the train reached the level crossing, she got up and stood by the door.

She stared in amazement and delight at the message "Stop and tork to me', spelt badly and written untidily, but heartrendingly readable.

One or two people on the train pointed, but her mother was nodding off and didn't see.

"Poor little mite," Emma heard someone say. "She wants the whole train to stop for her. How funny!"

The message wasn't for the whole train at all, it was for Emma. This was an invitation.

She stared as if a spaceship had landed and an alien had come out with a 'Take me to your leader' sign.

Alone that night Emma considered the message. This was a cry for help if ever there was one, and she wasn't going to ignore it. She would have to find a way to meet. They were almost twins, uncannily alike. They had to find out about each other, see what was happening between them.

The problem was how, and though she had avoided the shocking answer as long as possible, she faced it now.

She would play truant.

Never in a million years would she ever have thought she could do this. It was something others did in other schools, far away. No one did it in her school. Education was life and breath, interesting, demanding, vital. There was never a dull moment and it was as far from Grange Hill as her dad's fabulous stars were from Earth. It was one of the best schools in the country. Emma was the star pupil and there was never the faintest hint that she could be anything but super duper.

But Emma couldn't see any other alternative. Her time was monitored minute by minute with school and clubs and hobbies that she would never be able to find the hours she needed. Every evening there was something or other 'on' – athletics, gymnastics, riding, piano, singing – she was imprisoned in a timetable of wonderful opportunities, but she would drop them all to meet The Girl.

Emma tried reasoning with herself, arguing that she was being immature to consider ruining all she had worked for to meet a stranger who would probably disappoint anyway. She told herself over and over again not to let the idea of running off for a day take root, but it did, all the same. She felt The Girl's need greater than all the silent warnings clunking around in her mind.

She wondered what it would be like to break the rules. This wasn't just breaking the rules, though, it was a major ripping apart of everything her family held dear, trust and honesty most of all.

Over the next few days, the idea became a plan and overwhelmed her, so much so that it was evident to those who loved her that things weren't right.

One night, her mother said,

"Emma, Mrs. Sumner called today. She's worried about you. Said you're not performing to the best of your ability."

"I'm okay, mum."

"She also said some of the other teachers are a bit concerned, too, that you're not concentrating as hard as usual."

"I am."

"Well, they say you're not. Is anything bothering you, Emma?"

Emma realised that breaking the rules had consequences. Somehow, grown ups read in between the lines. They got messages from you, even if you didn't send them.

"No, nothing."

Silently, without knowing how, she'd gone beyond the pale.

She looked up timetables of trains from Cambridge to London. She worked out how to leave home normally for school, get to the station instead, take the train to Clapton, which was the closest point to where she'd seen The Girl, and what time train she'd have to catch to return home normally before anyone guessed what she'd done.

She thought she had enough trust at school to get away with it once, maybe twice, but once was all she needed. If they met, and they got on, then things could be dealt with differently, but just this once she could and would break the rules.

It was only just over an hour from Cambridge to London. There were quite a few trains, so it wasn't difficult. The hardest thing would be lying to everyone, mum and dad especially. Once she was sure of the times, she had to let The Girl know what she was going to do. She couldn't very well hold up a message from the train – everyone would see it. The message had to be secret, so she wrote a letter on paper :

"I will come to Clapton Station 11.20 on Monday. That's twenty past eleven. Your friend, Emma."

She folded it, put it in an envelope, wrapped the envelope around a stone and taped it down, then wrapped it in a plastic bag to protect it.

She felt like a spy and a traitor. She was hurting the dearest people in her life, but she'd decided she had no choice. The school would believe her story because she was Emma Chandler. She would just have to live with a little white lie for a while.

The following Saturday, she and her mother were on their way to London. Just before the train reached the level crossing, she went to the toilet where there was a narrow upper window which Emma pulled open. Standing on the seat, Emma threw the stone and watched it hit the ground near the level crossing and go rolling down the embankment. She peered out to see what she could see. Just before the train sped on, she caught sight of a figure emerging from a tunnel beneath the level crossing, a small, slight figure, heading towards the spot where the stone had fallen, not jogging, but, like a fragile young gazelle, leaping, dashing, elegantly ...

10   Train Ghost

"Running," said Emma, "I remember running."

The ghost listened intently, raised a wispy tendril of a finger and touched the window. A woman drifted into view.

"My teacher," said Emma, "Mrs ... Sum ..."

Names were locked away in the deep, dark prison of her mind, and it was all Emma could do not to cry with frustration because she couldn't free them. The ghost saw her anxiety.

"It'll be alright'," she said, "I know it will."

Emma put her head in her hand and banged it with her fists.

"Remember! Remember!" she told herself. "Stupid girl!" and then, with great relief, she said, "Mrs. Sumner! Sports Teacher. I ran races. I was good. I am good."

"Course you are! You're the best! An' I'll tell you somefing for nuffing. I'm good, too."

"You?"

The ghost bobbled as if it was chuckling to itself.

"Dunno if I'm good as you, but it would be great to run togever one day. Don't you fink? I didn't run no races. Just runnin' in the open, by meself. I liked that best. I was free, then, no one could touch me."

Emma felt the connection again. Something bound them. If only she could find the bond. A bridge, a train, a tunnel...

"You might have had an accident while you

were running," said Emma. "Was that how you died?"

The ghost didn't answer the question. Instead, it said, "You ain't listenin' to the troof, Emma Chandler. You ain't getting' to where you should be."

'Listening to the truth'. What did it mean? Emma saw herself running on a track. She felt a sense of freedom, as if running were more natural than walking. A picture popped into her mind of a girl throwing something out of a window and another girl running for it.

Always running.

"Were you a champion?" Emma asked the ghost.

The ghost laughed.

"Me? Champion Stupid Girl."

"You shouldn't say that. You sound clever to me."

The ghost was quiet for a moment. It seemed touched by Emma's comment.

"I ain't clever. Never was. Never will be."

"Well you sound it. But you ran, like me?"

"I ran. Like you."

Emma looked at the image in the window, touched it and it vanished. Other memories of school and family vanished with it.

"We're not the same person, are we?" she asked. "You're not the ghost of me?"

The ghost laughed again.

"No. I couldn't be you. You're smart."

Emma wished she was smart enough to understand what was going on.

"There were races," she said, "I thought they were important, but they weren't, not compared to this," and she gestured to the empty train. "I won them, though, so I must have been alright."

"You were more than alight," said the ghost. "And you're remembering 'em. Thas great. You're gonna be okay, I know it."

"Is there something wrong with me, then, ghost? Won't you tell me if there is?"

The ghost oozed compassion and concern.

"Stop the train an' I'll tell you everyfing. Honest."

Emma believed the ghost, but still wouldn't or couldn't do it. Besides, the stop button looked suddenly very far away, hard to reach.

"Perhaps you better do it without me," she said. "Let me sleep now. I'm sure I'll be fine. It's nice of you to keep me company like this, but you must have other people to haunt."

"I ain't haunting," the ghost replied urgently. "Don't you see, I mustn't let you go, I can't let you go, I won't let you go! I dunno much about meself, and I dunno less about you, but I know one fing, and thas an important fing, the most' important fing of all, and thas … thas you're my …"

11   Emmy in Trouble

"Friend!" shouted Emmy as she struggled to read the message wrapped around the stone. "I gotta friend! I gotta friend!"

She'd spent an hour trying to decipher the message thrown from the train, and she'd done it! Now she knew The Girl's name.

And it was Emma!

That's what it had to be, because they looked like each other they had to have names like each other. She'd known it all along.

Emmy was almost dancing around the marshes.

She couldn't believe Emma was going to come and see her! They'd be real friends! Emma would teach her how to read and write and everything would be good from now on.

She checked the message over and over and fixed the meeting time in her memory. Monday. Twenty past eleven. Clapton Station. She was so proud that she'd understood the message. She would have liked to check it with someone, but there was no one she trusted. It just had to be right. 'Your friend, Emma.' Emmy repeated the words. No one had ever said, 'Your Friend', '*Your* friend'.

She stared at the note as if she was afraid it might suddenly vanish. It was proof that she wasn't alone any more. She felt a moment of panic in case Emma would see how stupid she was and hate her. But that couldn't happen! It would be too cruel!

She sat beneath the level crossing and studied

the note, reading, thinking, making plans.

Monday. She ought to be at school. But then, Emma should be at school, too. It didn't matter a jot to Emmy whether she was at school or not, but Emma was different. Emmy worried that she was getting her new friend into trouble, but still she couldn't help but be excited.

Emmy was different, too. All the other girls at school had friends but Emmy was always alone, tackling the world by herself. Deep down, though, cocooned but aching to be free, she knew there was a beautiful butterfly waiting to take wing and astonish the world, if only, if only!

She checked the time. Late! She'd get into trouble! Ah, but she didn't care! She looked at the note, afraid it might have disappeared in a puff of imagination. It was there, real as could be, and the words shone through like some angel in heaven. 'Your friend, Emma'.

She folded the note carefully, put it in a pocket and decided that, as she was late already, she'd be even later, and ran around the edge of the marshes, taking the long way home. She didn't care much about her father or his nasty friends. The only thing that mattered was that she had sent a message and the message had been answered.

Her feet hardly touched the ground. She flew along, believing there was no one her age on Earth who could catch her or match her. She didn't worry about being told off at school, at home, anywhere, because someone had at last noticed her and there was hope. Her heart beat faster. She felt elated. If this worked, they could meet regularly, Emma could make her clever, she wouldn't be so shy and angry any more, she'd understand things that had always confused her, everything and everybody would make sense and people like Saul and Victor, and even dad, yes dad, wouldn't matter any more.

Two days, less than two days, that was all there was before they met!

She reached home determined that neither dad nor his dangerous friends would spoil her mood. She started to open the door and immediately it was flung open and her father grabbed her by her collar, swearing.

"Where the blazes you been, Emmy?"

She just stared at him. His eyes were red, his face flushed.

"Nowhere," she whispered.

He pulled her inside and raised his hand to strike her, but a voice from behind ordered him, very quietly but firmly, to stop. Emmy saw Saul, tall and lanky, a spectre, standing behind her father, his face the usual mask of callous coldness and hidden venom.

"Leave it," he said. "Just bring her in."

Her father pushed her into the living room where Victor was sitting at the table, papers spread out in front of him. He turned as Emmy was deposited on the shabby sofa.

"Well, look what the cat's dragged in!" he laughed. "Your dad's been worried sick, Emmy. You should be ashamed of yourself."

Emmy wasn't ashamed of herself at all. She didn't believe her father had been worried sick at all, he was just in a foul mood.

"Calm down, Will," said Victor. "No point in losing your cool. You gotta do as you're told, Emmy," he said.

Emmy sat on the sofa staring at him. Who was he to tell her what to do? It was none of his business. This was her house!

She tried to calm herself, not to let these men spoil her mood. She felt the message in her pocket and remembered her new and good friend.

"How would you like to earn yourself some dosh, Emmy?" asked Victor, looking at Emmy.

Emmy shrugged, saying nothing.

"Answer the man," said her father, still angry, partly from her being late, but mainly at his own weakness and guilt, getting her involved in the wrong kind of life.

"Don't," she said, fearing what she might have to do to earn it.

Victor laughed. Saul stared, impassively. Her father cringed.

"Well, young Em," said Victor, "You must be the only one in the world to turn down money. What have you taught her, Will?"

Emmy's father scowled and turned away.

"Don't you know what money is?" asked Victor. "Money is the blood of the world. You should know that as soon as you can, Em. Money doesn't just make the world go around, it is the world. With it, you're everything, without it, you're nothing. Simple as that."

Emmy didn't want to listen because anything that came out of the mouths of these men was a lie, but she had no choice.

"That's what life is, little Emmy," said Victor. "Life is getting rich, any way you can. And that's what we're going to do. People like us, Em, you too, born with nothing. Work hard, nothing. Try hard, nothing. Don't matter what we do, nothing. The world spits at us because we're poor. Treats us like we're not worth the space we stand on, because we're poor. Spouts a whole load of words, but all lies, Emmy, all lies."

Emmy didn't want to listen even if some of what he was saying was true. She wanted to think about Monday, but she was getting a creeping, sickening feeling in her stomach that everything was going to go horribly wrong.

"Look at you, Em," Victor went on, "and your poor old dad, not a penny to your names. Look at your clothes, like rags. Not because your father doesn't love you, because he does, in his own way, but because he doesn't have the cash to buy you nice clothes like all your friends have. Isn't that right? Look at me, tough old boot, given my life to hard work, and poor as a church mouse. You see, Em, the world is for the rich. Always was, always will be. No money, no nothing. You can be nice as pie, and you are a nice girl, Emmy, we can all see that, but nice will get you a big fat zero."

Emmy tried to close her ears.

"You ever cut yourself, Em?" Victor asked. "Sure you have, and what happens, you bleed. Blood. And what happens if you lose too much blood, you die. You ever choked on anything, Em? What happens when you choke, you can't breathe and you die. You know what I'm getting at? These things is life, Emmy, blood and air. Can't live without them. Now though you don't think so, money's the same. Can't live without money. You don't have money, you suffocate and die. You don't have money, you bleed to death and die."

Emmy hated Victor for telling her all this. It

71

might or might not be true, but she didn't want to hear it.

"We've been thinking, your dad, me and Saul, and we've been planning. But we need your help, Emmy."

"Me? Why?"

That was the first thing she'd said for ages. Victor had made her nervous. What help could she be? She didn't want to get involved in their stupid plans, not now, even if money was the blood of life or whatever Victor had said it was.

"Because you're like us, Emmy, you're one of us. We know you're just a kid and all that, but Will, your dad, he said you could do this and we think you could, too."

"Do what?"

Emmy suddenly hated her father again for mixing her up in this, whatever 'this' turned out to be, though she guessed 'this' was going to be a crime and a disaster.

"I'll tell you, but first I wanted you to know why it's important. You're a clever little thing and you understand, right?"

She understood. All that rubbish about money was just so that they could ask her – tell her - to help them do whatever terrible thing they were planning to do. She nodded that she understood.

"We've been waiting on you, Emmy," Victor went on, "almost two hours, which is why your dad's a bit uppity."

Her dad wasn't uppity, he was furious.

"Time is important when you plan this kind of thing," he said. "Can't have you keeping us waiting when we really need you," and he tapped his watch.

"What d'you want me to do?" asked Emmy, hoping whatever it was wouldn't be dangerous and, more important, wouldn't be on Monday. Monday was her time and not dad, Saul nor Victor was going to mess it up for her.

"First thing we want you to do," said Victor, "is to believe in us."

Emmy stared. What did he mean?

"You're growing up," said Victor, "soon be a young woman, but your head's full of stories. Just because you're poor," he went on, "and bottom of the pile, doesn't mean magic happens and you get rich and happy and famous. Don't expect no wardrobe to let you into some stupid land," he said, "because it won't because there isn't one. Don't expect no prince to come and kiss you and abracadabra everything's alright, because there is no prince. Don't expect no magic, none whatsoever, Emmy, because magic is nonsense. The sooner you put such things out of your head and understand the real world, the happier you'll be. Which is why you have to believe in us. Do you believe in us?" he asked.

"Dunno," whispered Emmy.

"Told you she'd be difficult," said her father, still angry, still uncomfortable with himself.

"Dunno isn't an answer," said Victor. "Am I telling the truth, Emmy, or not?"

Emmy shrugged.

"What d'you want me to do?" she repeated.

The three men looked at each other. They obviously had a plan, Emmy had known that for weeks. They'd been meeting and talking and discussing things almost every day. At first they hadn't wanted her to

73

know, but now she had to know because she was going to be involved.

"I'm asking you, Emmy," said Victor, "because I want to know if I can trust you, if *we* can trust you. You see, if you do it, that means you're going to know things, and if you know things, you can get us in trouble as well as help us. You see what I mean?"

She did.

"Now, if you know what you're doing and you see why you're doing it and you know it's the right and only thing for people like us and people like you to do, then I think we can trust you more than if we just bully you. Isn't that right, Emmy?"

Emmy felt bullied. She was too scared to get up and tell these three bullies to leave her alone, which is what she wanted to do. It seemed like Victor wanted her heart as well as her time, and she couldn't give him that, but what could she say or do besides kick and scream?

"S'ppose so," she muttered.

"Good," said Victor. "Because once we tell you, there's no untelling. You understand?"

"Yeh."

"Come and sit at the table, Emmy, be one of us."

Emmy got up from the sofa and sat at the table, next to Victor. Her heart was beating fast because she was nervous. She would rather be anywhere on Earth than there, and yet the day had promised so much, in fact it had promised everything. She'd wanted to read and reread the note from Emma and to think about Monday morning, what they would do, where they could go and how their friendship would be the best thing ever. But here she was, sitting with three crooks, including her father, listening to them explain how they could get away with a whole bucket load of money if only she helped them. She was almost thirteen years old and she was going to be a criminal.

"She's thick, I told you," growled her father when she didn't say much. Emmy looked at him in contempt and he couldn't look back.

Victor was unexpectedly patient and went over the details as many times as Emmy needed.

Later, when she knew all there was to know and the two men had gone, she lay in bed, unable to sleep, her head split between the hope she'd had a few hours before and the unhappiness she felt now. She couldn't understand how her father could ask her to do this. The only thing she imagined was that he was scared, not of her, of course, but of Saul and Victor. Especially Saul. Saul never said anything, but looked as if he could hurt without conscience. He gave Emmy the creeps and perhaps he gave her father the creeps, too. The only other possibility was that her father hated her, blamed her for the mess their lives were in and for everything that ever went wrong. She felt as if she'd been an accident, not a child wanted and loved.

She could have said no to the plan, but the pressure the three men put on her was enormous and she felt that even if they got caught, she wouldn't be blamed and go to prison or anything because people would know it wasn't her choice or her fault. She would have said no if the plan had been for Monday morning, but it wasn't. When she'd asked and Victor had told her "tomorrow night, Sunday" she'd tried to hide her relief. She could do the stupid thing they wanted her to do and then meet Emma the next morning. She might even tell her what she'd done, what she'd had to do, although she

75

didn't want to scare her away.

It was midnight and she still couldn't sleep. She went to the kitchen and took a glass of milk. She could hear her father snoring. He stopped for a moment and Emmy waited, then he started again and she relaxed, drinking the milk and wandering into the living room.

Papers had been left on the table.

She looked again at the plan of the house, the front door, the rear garden door, the downstairs rooms, the staircase, the upstairs bedrooms. Victor had indicated the safe with an 'X', just like a treasure map.

She wondered if she should take the map to the police, but she daren't. When Victor and Saul found out, which they would, they'd kill her. Really kill her. And she couldn't cheat on her dad. She loved him and hated him at the same time, and though he'd got her into something bad and dangerous, she just couldn't sneak to the police behind his back. She'd do this terrible thing and it would be over. "No one's going to get hurt, love," Victor had reassured her, "we're just going to redistribute the wealth of the world a little," which made Victor laugh, her father smile and Saul sneer.

Emmy went back to bed, wishing that she could be clever and strong and knew what to do. She wished her dad would tell Victor and Saul to leave them alone, that his beloved daughter wasn't going to get into trouble for them and that they should never talk to her again. She wished a hundred good things that wouldn't happen and tried not to think of all the bad things that probably would.

Somehow, the joy and excitement of Emma's message had got lost in the threat from Victor and Saul and the crime they wanted her to commit.

She fell asleep in the early hours, dreaming of trains and windows, of friends and enemies, of Victor and Saul and her own pathetic father. In her hand, clenched tightly, even in sleep, she held the note, squeezing it as if it was the most important thing in the world, and it was. It was freedom for the butterfly. She was surrounded by paths of despair, selfishness and cruelty, but in her hand she held a tiny sliver of hope, generosity and kindness, all delicately balanced, quietly fighting a silent war to ...

12   Emma in Trouble

" 'The End'," said Emma, putting down the picture book she'd been reading to Benjy. At four years old, Benjy soaked up stories like a sponge and never so much so as when they were read to him by his big sister. Emma was The One. He chuckled when he saw her, jumped on her when she arrived, clung to her when she left. Her voice was the centre of his little world and she could do no wrong by him.

"How big is the world, Emma?" he asked.

"Very big. Too big to measure, Ben. She couldn't really do it, you know."

The girl in the story had tried to measure everything there was in the world, people, places, feelings. It had made Benjy think, and more surprisingly, it had made Emma think, too.

Benjy was as much the light of her life as she was of his, and she felt she was about to let him down. Until now, Emma had played by the rules, doing what was expected, what was right. She'd never done anything as bad as playing truant. It was as crazy a thing to do as trying to measure the world with a ruler. Emma hoped that no one, least of all Benjy, would find out, but she suspected that somehow, for some stupid reason, what she was about to do would be found out and everyone would know, yet no one be able to explain.

Even she couldn't explain it. She just felt compelled to meet this mysterious twin who had called out to her for help. How could she refuse?

"Benjy?"

Benjy looked up from his tiny bed. Emma asked him a simple but important question,

"Do you think I'm a bad girl?"

Benjy laughed and said, "Yes," then carried on giggling as if it were the silliest question and silliest answer.

Emma pressed him more.

"I know I'm not bad all the time, but if I did something wrong once, would I be bad forever?"

Benjy didn't understand.

"Would you still love me, Benjy, if I did something wrong?"

Benjy stopped giggling and asked, "What are you going to do, Emma?"

Emma stroked Benjy's hair and replied, "Nothing terrible. Maybe nothing at all. Just want to know if you'll love me forever."

"No," said Benjy, quickly, and started giggling all over again.

"You know something, Benjy," Emma said to her little brother, "you're hopeless and useless."

"Hopeness and usetass," Benjy tried to repeat.

"You're a waste of baby space,"

"Wait for baby's face!"

"You're a lump of lard."

"Lumpelard."

"And I love you."

Benjy giggled hysterically. Their mother came in, saw the two laughing and said, "You're supposed to be reading him to sleep, Emma."

"Sleep!" repeated Benjy, now in full repetitive mode.

"Sorry," said Emma.

"Emma bad sister," said Benjy and dived under the bedclothes.

Their mother looked at Emma and asked, "Why did he say that?"

Emma shrugged.

"Because he's a silly little baby," she said, and poked the squirming shape of her little brother. Benjy stuck his head out and said,

"Emma said she was bad."

Emma wished she hadn't said a word.

"Oh?" her mother asked, "I don't think so, Benjy. Did you say that, Em?"

"I was joking," Emma replied. "Just wanted to know if Benjy loved me, and she prodded him again, hoping they could change the subject. Benjy wouldn't let it go, though.

"Emma bad, Emma bad, Emma bad!" and then he giggled furiously until his mother told him to settle down, pulled the bedclothes up to his neck, kissed him goodnight and turned off the light with instructions to sleep straight away.

"That was a funny thing to say, Emma," she said when they were downstairs in the lounge. "Or was he making it all up?"

Emma tried to hide her discomfort and said Benjy was just being silly.

"You haven't been yourself, lately, though," her mother said. "Anything bothering you? Growing up things, maybe?"

Emma shook her head.

"No. I'm fine."

"Best not to keep things in," said her mother.

"Always good to share problems."

"No, really. I'm alright."

She wasn't, though. The idea of truanting had turned into the equivalent of murder, it seemed such a terrible thing to do.

She played a game of Scrabble with her mother; her dad was busy in his study and Cal was out with yet another new girlfriend. Emma knew she was about to betray everyone who loved and trusted her. She ought to have left the subject alone, but she couldn't. She had to dig a little.

"Mum?"

Her mother looked up from a rack of seven impossible letters.

"Yes?"

"Did you do anything wrong when you were a girl?"

"Of course I did. Everyone does. Why, love?"

"Just wondered."

"Have you done anything, Em, I mean, a serious something?"

"No. What did you do?"

Her mother thought hard, trying to recollect some minor misdemeanours.

"Nothing heavy, Emma. The usual things people do. Never went to prison or anything like that, if that's what you mean."

Emma smiled, but she was struggling with guilt and anxiety. Could she really go ahead with this stupid idea? Should she go ahead with it? It would be such a relief to talk with someone about it, get another opinion, share the responsibility, but she couldn't. If she told her mother, the answer would assuredly be 'no'. She wouldn't be in trouble, but she'd be failing The Girl and that she just couldn't do.

"What's the worst thing you've ever done?" she asked.

"Not sure I've ever done anything that bad," her mother replied, and then, "but sometimes things seem terrible at the time, nothing a little later. Look, Em, I don't want to press you, but something's obviously worrying you. Can't you tell me?"

She couldn't. Her mother tried to reassure her.

"Darling, whatever it is, we'll always love you. I can't believe you're up to anything seriously serious, it's not like you, and I don't think you could do it anyway. You know right from wrong without asking, so perhaps it's like I said, things seeming worse than they are. Growing up isn't easy, you know."

Emma knew that, though she also knew she'd had things easy, in comparison. She felt this was an opportunity to do something good, even if it also meant doing something bad first. The end would justify the means. Oh, why were decisions so difficult! It would be much easier if they were clear, do this, right, do that, wrong, end of story. But right and wrong overlapped and you couldn't seem to do one thing without doing the other.

Sunday was a busy day, but not busy enough to stop her worrying. In the morning she had a piano lesson with Ms. Gryst. Piano lessons were never bundles of fun and Ms. Gryst was a hard teacher. She insisted on perfect technique, hands poised at the right angle, wrists suitably flexed, fingers well positioned, back straight and so on. She also insisted on endless scales, not just the regular major and minors, but modes, too, and some jazz scales thrown in. She enjoyed studies which were Emma's idea of hell and never left a scale, a study or a piece alone until it was note perfect. Emma was one of her best pupils, a natural talent if Ms. Gryst had ever heard one. It was therefore that much more surprising when Emma made a complete hash of her three part invention.

"Emma?"

"Yes, I know."

"Have you been practising?"

Ms. Gryst never asked this question to Emma because she knew as sure as eggs were eggs that Emma had been practising. She had this week, too, and said so.

"Then what's the matter?"

"I'm doing my best."

Doing one's best was not a phrase Ms. Gryst liked. She wanted her students to excel because she reflected in their glory and Emma was one of her most potentially glorious students. Doing one's best meant average, and average wasn't a word in Ms. Gryst's vocabulary.

"It isn't good enough, Emma. Not like you at all. You look preoccupied. Try to focus more."

Focus was Emma's strong point, so she felt suddenly quite vulnerable not being able to concentrate.

"I'm trying!"

"Alright. I'm not telling you off, Emma. Just want the best from you. Play the left hand only. Keep it steady. Bach is nothing if not steady. Go."

She couldn't do it.

"Count as you play, one, two, three, four, one, two, three, four, one...go."

"...two, three, four, one..."

The only thing playing on Emma's mind was Monday, imagining herself on the train to London, betraying parents, friends, teachers.

"No, no, Emma. You're all over the place. Count!"

Emma counted, but her fingers were disconnected from the counting. Ms. Gryst switched on a metronome but Emma found herself listening to the endless tick, tick, tick as if it was counting down to her foolish adventure. She felt like a criminal. Her parents would be furious with her, not just angry but furious, and they were never that.

The piano lesson seemed to last forever. The music sounded distant and difficult, as if someone else was playing. Ms. Gryst was puzzled and disappointed. She looked forward to Emma's lessons and thought that perhaps Emma was going the same way as many of her adolescent pupils, into the void of a non-musical life.

Back home, Emma sat with her family for Sunday lunch.

"How was piano?" her father asked.

"Okay."

"What are you playing?" Cal asked, Cal who had got Grade 8 at sixteen years but gave it all up for love, as he put it, foolishness, as his mother put it.

Emma had to think. She could hardly remember the lesson, now. When she told him, he said,

"Bach, right. Three part inventions – does your head in, Emma. No wonder you're looking a bit dazed."

"Am I?"

It was hard to hide a secret. It wasn't just a matter of keeping quiet, you had to change your face, your looks, your mood, your mind, everything.

Impossible.

"When you think about it," said Cal, "three part inventions aren't natural. We only have one brain and it can only do one thing at a time, not two, definitely not three. The man was obviously an alien."

"Who?"

"Bach. Think about it, multi-brain music, he couldn't have been human."

Benjy, who was sitting in a high chair, giggled away as if his big brother had said the funniest thing, but Cal could say anything, even recite the dictionary, and Benjy would have laughed. He adored Cal almost as much as he adored Emma.

"Interesting theory," said Mr. Chandler. "So, basically, anyone who comes up with something above the ordinary is an alien? You've been watching too much television, Calum."

Emma listened to the conversation and the jokes as if they were on stage and she were a dull audience. Her plan weighed on her and imprisoned her. All she wanted was to cry and confess, but she couldn't do either.

In the afternoon she went riding. Her horse, Sparky, felt there was something wrong and looked at her with eyes that were slightly more doleful than usual. On the other hand, her riding partner chatted away relentlessly, noticing nothing, which proved to Emma that animals could be far more sensitive to moods than some humans.

She had a couple of hours homework to do in the evening and was struggling over the binomial theorem when there was a knock on the door and her father came in.

"Busy?" he asked.

She shook her head and held back her tears. She was co close to confessing!

Mr. Chandler sat on the edge of Emma's bed and asked what she was doing.

"Maths was never my strong point," he said, when she showed him, "but you can't do science without it. Press on, old girl."

He paused a moment, then said, "My lovely Emma, you're growing up, and growing up isn't exactly a doddle. If there's something bothering you, you can talk to mum or me, you know that?"

"I know. Thanks."

"We wouldn't ever blame you. We love you. We don't like to see you upset, and you are a bit, aren't you?"

"A bit."

"Anything you can tell your dad?"

Now was her chance, probably her last chance. They all knew she was troubled, but they couldn't read her mind. 'Tell him, tell him!' a voice urged her, but she didn't, she just shook her head, slowly. The inner voice faded, leaving echoes of sadness.

Mr. Chandler stood up and stroked Emma's hair.

"You're our darling daughter," he said, "our one and only. When you're hurt, we're hurt. You know that?"

She did.

"And you know that you can share anything with us, absolutely anything, don't you?"

She did that, too.

"But we don't press," he went on. "We trust you. And whatever you do, we know it will be the right thing.

Okay?"

Okay, and not okay.

The word 'trust' cut to her heart. That's what she was doing, breaking their trust, and once broken it might never be mended.

But still she kept quiet.

Strangely, she slept well. There were dreams, but not the terrible ones she'd feared.

Monday morning was bright and clear.

She put on her school uniform, went through the usual morning rituals automatically, as if she'd been programmed to behave one way, to think another, then started out for school. At a safe enough distance from home she turned, called a friend on her mobile to say she wasn't well and wasn't going in that day, took a detour and walked, each heavy step weighed with guilt and conscience, towards the ...

13   Train Ghost

"Station!" Emma exclaimed, "there was a station!"

The ghost hung on to every word Emma's said and each time Emma recovered scraps of memory, the ghost cajoled her for more, encouraging, helping, always gently drawing out more recollections.

This time, the memory vanished before Emma could seize it.

She slumped back, terribly tired. Her eyes felt lead heavy, as if she hadn't slept for days and as if she could make up for it now by sleeping for a month. Endless attempts at remembering the things that had fallen from her mind exhausted her.

"Better not sleep now," said the ghost. "Fings to fink about."

For all its odd way of speaking, the ghost's voice was indisputably comforting and Emma would have felt so lonely without it. Nevertheless, she didn't yet understand its reason for being there.

"Are you helping or bothering me?" she asked. "What difference does it make to you?"

The ghost replied, "We're friends, thas the difference."

"Friends," Emma whispered. "Are we? How come?"

If the ghost was truly helping her, she didn't know why, and she couldn't offer help in return - the ghost was dead and it didn't matter what Emma did, she couldn't bring it back to life.

"Because thas the way it is," the ghost said. "There ain't an explanation for everyfing."

Also without an explanation were the visions which Emma saw through the train window. If she didn't know better, she'd say the ghost conjured them up itself. Visions appeared now - a man, a woman, a young man and a little boy. They were sitting at a table, eating, but quietly and without joy.

"Who are they?" the ghost asked.

"My family," Emma replied, staring at them with a full heart. This was her fault! If it wasn't for her, they would be happy! She felt as if she'd done something unforgivably wrong to make them all so serious and sad, only she didn't know what she'd done. If only she could remember! All she wanted now was to be back with them, to be the fifth one at the table and change their sadness to laughter.

"Why are you showing me this?" she asked.

"S'to make you live again," said the ghost. "Wish I 'ad a family like that," it went on, "You're lucky."

Lucky? Emma didn't think so. She felt massively unlucky, and guilty, as if she'd done something she shouldn't have done, been somewhere she shouldn't have been, but it was all distant, like looking through the wrong end of a pair of binoculars.

"What were they like, your mum and dad?" the ghost asked. "And your big bruvver, what was he like?"

"Like?" Emma repeated. "They were … kind … yes … and my big brother … he was … Head Boy … yes … and my little brother …do you know his name, ghost? … I miss him so much … I wish I could be with them again."

"You will," the ghost answered. "Tell us about 'em."

Emma couldn't take her eyes off the vision in the window. The ghost wanted to know everything there was to know and Emma did her best to tell what she could. It helped enormously to talk about these people who she knew she once had loved, and still did, in a vague and vanishing kind of way.

The ghost never tired. It asked endless questions and waited with unfeigned interest for the answers. Emma even laughed. The ghost was funny and affectionate, not at all the spooky thing Emma had first feared. Now, Emma recognised its kindness and generosity.

She turned away from the window for a moment and when she turned back the image of her family was gone. Nothing replaced it, just the dismal, heart wrenching void. She wanted so much to sleep, not to see that emptiness any more, but there were voices calling her, not least the ghost's, who made her think of her life, her family, her friends. Emma had the feeling the ghost knew the answers to almost all these questions, but she played along because, for some reason she didn't understand, she trusted it, even though it refused, or wasn't able, to answer questions. It was there purely to help Emma remember.

"Fink!" said the ghost, again and again.

"I am 'finking'," Emma replied, again and again.

When it came to the puzzle of the empty train, Emma had memories of being on a train with her mother, but also one of being on it without her.

"By yourself?" the ghost asked.

"I think so. Yes. I … I was going to meet someone."

"Who?" the ghost asked, anxiously.

Emma couldn't find a name.

"I don't think I've forgotten," she said. "I don't think I even knew. But then, why would I be meeting someone I never knew? I must be wrong."

The ghost told Emma she wasn't wrong, that everything she remembered was right and that she could remember more if she tried harder. Emma said,

"I might remember more, ghost, if I could see you better. It's not easy talking to you like this, you know."

The ghost fidgeted, then said,

"Just to 'elp you, yeh, okay. Let's see what 'appens. But you'll have to do the 'ard work."

"Hard work? Well, I'll try, although I'm so sleepy, ghost … alright, go on then."

"Ready?"

"Ready."

The ghost stood silent for a few seconds, as if gathering its energy.

"I 'ad green eyes," it said.

And at once, weirdly and wonderfully, Emma saw two distinct green eyes appear in the ghostly shape. They weren't at all scary, just very beautiful.

The ghost saw Emma stare at her.

"I can see them!" cried Emma. "Your eyes! I can see them!"

The ghost put its grey, wispy tendrils up to its face but it was like a cloud sweeping into another cloud.

"More!" Emma said, growing excited.

The ghost screwed up its peculiar white face, but

nothing happened.

"Thas all," it said.

"No!" exclaimed Emma, disappointed. "You have to show me more. I know you can! What colour hair did you have? What colour skin? How tall were you?"

The ghost hesitated, studying Emma first, then said,

"'bout your height, 'bout like you in loads o' ways, I fink."

Like you! How could this shifting, foggy thing have been like her?

"Was it a long time ago?" Emma asked.

"No. Wasn't a long time ago."

"Show me what you looked like," Emma insisted, her sleepiness set aside for a while.

"I had black 'air," said the ghost, "like yours."

And as soon as she said this, it happened again. Emma could see a hint of black amidst the foggy ghostliness.

"What colour skin did you have?" Emma asked.

"Pink," said the ghost, "like yours."

At once, Emma made out colours in the spectral mist. Pink here and there, little hands, and a face. Emma stared as if she were looking at a magic trick. She was fascinated. The ghost rose and fell, as if alive and breathing, its new pinkness and blackness rising with it, a half human trapped inside a half ghost.

Something jolted inside Emma.

"Can't you remember what you were wearing?" Emma asked, urgently and quietly.

The ghost became still, its eyes closing for a few moments. When they opened again, it said,

"I fink so," and there were a pair of loose fitting old jeans, a blank white t-shirt and two dull trainers covering a pair of bright red socks.

Ever so slowly the ghost dissolved, and in its place sat a little ghost-girl.

But not just any girl.

Emma found herself looking into what was almost a mirror image.

Almost.

The ghost was astonishingly similar to Emma, but smaller and frailer.

"You're me!" Emma whispered, disbelieving.

"And you're me," said the ghost. "Only you ain't really. And I ain't you. We just look like each uvver. I ain't ugly, am I?" it asked.

Emma shook her head.

"If you are, so am I. We're like twins! Who are you, ghost? Won't you tell me your name?"

The ghost closed its eyes and squeezed its thin hands. Its face was stone still as if it was arguing with itself.

"Can't," it answered.

"You can't? Why not?"

"Becoz you know it already," the ghost said.

Emma dug deep as midnight to remember. When she did, her face relaxed and the ghost knew she knew.

Emma had made the connection.

"You!" she cried. "I know you! Your name is …"

14 Emmy's Crime

"Emmy," said dad, "I know you don't want to do this, but …"

"I don't!" Emmy interrupted. "So why should I?"

It was Sunday evening and she'd had two days to think about their stupid plan and she resented being part of it more now than ever. She had the sickening feeling that things were going to go horribly wrong. Her father stood in the doorway to her bedroom, ill at ease. He couldn't deal with her like this, and yet there was no way he could tell Saul and Victor that Emmy wasn't coming – they needed her.

"They'll hurt you, that's why."

"Don't care."

She did care, of course. She was terrified of Saul and Victor and was angry at her father for letting them push him around. She'd had plenty of time to think about it, and though at first she thought she'd do what they wanted – just to be free of them again - she'd gradually become more and more nervous. Now, at the twelfth hour, she'd decided against it. Her father was close to panicking.

"You will care, Em. God knows what those two might do to you … to us."

"And you'd let them, wouldn't you?"

Emmy thought less of her father than she'd ever done. Who would protect her if even her father was too cowardly to help? No one. Emma probably had more courage than him. And it was the thought of meeting her that made her sit tight and not co-operate. Meeting Emma was going to be the best thing that ever happened to her and she wasn't going to let these selfish criminals spoil it. It wasn't fair and Emmy wouldn't do it.

"Em, I wouldn't ask you to do this if it weren't for a good reason," he told her. "You heard what Victor said about money. He's right, love. Without money you got nothing in this world, and that's what we've got, nothing. I ain't got enough to pay rent, pay the bills, buy you things, Emmy, which is what I would do. Life's just not fair and you have to do things sometimes you don't want to do. This ain't dangerous, love…"

"Hah!" exclaimed Emmy. She couldn't think of anything more dangerous.

"…I wouldn't ask you to do anything really risky."

Of course he would. He would ask her to jump off a cliff if he thought he'd get rich. Nothing mattered to him or to his friends except money. No wonder mum left him.

Emmy sat silent on the bed, determined not to go. Her father persisted,

"I promise I'll never ask you to do nothing again. This is a doddle, Emmy. Victor wouldn't tell us to do this if it weren't. I know you don't like him…"

"I hate him."

"..or Saul…"

"…I hate him more.

"Right, but they're our sort, love, they're our friends. They're my friends. We met in, well, you know…."

"Prison!" Emmy spat at him.

"Alright, prison. We get on. We trust each other.

You gotta trust them, too. Just this once."

Emma didn't trust them at all, not this once, not ever. It wasn't as if they had some master plan to rob the bank of England with high tech James Bond type stuff, they hadn't. They were just small time crooks with big ideas and hardly a brain to share between them. They would get her and her dad into big trouble and that was the only thing she believed about this whole sorry business.

She crossed her legs on the bed and folded her arms tightly around herself; she was the only one who could give herself comfort. Her father stood still, looking hard at his stubborn daughter, but it didn't matter how hard he stared, she wouldn't budge, and she certainly wouldn't trust Saul or Victor, ever.

Stalemate.

They might have stayed like this for much longer, but the sound of a door opening and closing broke the silence.

"I gave them the key," Emmy's father said, quietly.

Emmy looked at him as if he were the stupidest man on Earth. He'd given Saul and Victor a key to their home! They didn't even have to knock any more, they could come and go as they pleased! What a fool!

Emmy heard the familiar voice of Victor call out,

"You there, Will?"

Emmy's father answered, "In here!"

Emmy looked at him in astonishment. He was virtually telling these two crazy men to come into her bedroom!

Victor looked around the door.

"Ready?" he asked.

It was getting late. They had to prepare and leave. Victor's good humour had gone and in its place was a serious and frightening determination. He was a man who liked to get his own way, and quickly.

"Emmy doesn't want to do it," said Emmy's father.

Emmy expected Victor to try and persuade her, and she was prepared for more arguments, but he didn't. Instead, he turned to Saul who came in to the room, paused for a moment, stood in front of Emmy and without warning lifted his hand and smacked her across the face, a wide, flowing and cracking slap that knocked her sideways.

Emmy's cheek stung and her will power cracked and broke. She looked up at Saul and saw for sure what kind of a man he was, a bully and a thug. Her father objected weakly, but Victor held his hand up to stop further dissent.

Emmy caught Saul's eyes and they held her, like a rabbit in headlights. She'd never seen a face like that with eyes like that. It seemed to Emmy that there was only cruelty, no heart, no soul, no love, nothing but cruelty. He scared her more than she thought it was possible to be scared and all the fight left her.

Victor spoke and said, "Emmy, sweetheart, there's no time for playacting. Get dressed, two minutes. Okay?"

She nodded.

Saul and Victor left the room. Her father waited a moment, looking at her with apologetic eyes, but she turned away.

They drove to the house, about fifteen miles

away. As they drove, Victor talked about the 'job'.

"First of many, Emmy, if this goes well. Remember the layout, three floors and a basement, TV room at the top, kitchen and dining room on the second, bedrooms on the ground, spare rooms and study in the basement. Got it?"

Emmy's job was to get through a tiny louver window which Victor told her was poorly locked. A louver window was made up of narrow glass slats bound by metal strips. They were levered open on the inside to let in air, but weren't that difficult to push open from the outside. The couple who lived in the house hadn't put good locks on the window and Victor, eyes like a hawk, saw the opportunity. However, even if you slid out all the slats, only someone very small and skinny could get in, and that meant Emmy.

They reached the house which was in a posh street in a posh area. It was dark and quiet with just a few people around. When the car was parked they got out and walked towards the house. Emmy wanted to run off. She knew she could, because none of the men would be able to catch her, but she had nowhere to go. There was no one interested in her, except Emma. Besides, she feared what Saul would do to her, or her father, if she ran away and ruined their plans.

There were spacious gardens around the house, enclosed by a six foot wall. They went around the back. Victor nodded to Saul who held his hands out. Emmy's father stood on them, then clambered over the wall and dropped to the other side. Victor motioned to Emmy. She stood on Saul's hands, her heart pounding, but she climbed over, too, into her father's arms. She pushed him away and waited.

"Sorry, love," her father started to say, "I…", but Emmy shook her head in anger and took a few steps away from him.

Victor came next, then Saul, by himself, tall and strong enough to climb over without help.

They looked around. Emmy recognised the house from Victor's drawings and wondered how he'd got to know it in such detail – perhaps he had worked there or knew someone who had worked there.

Saul, Victor and her father slipped on black balaclavas which hid their faces. Her father gave one to Emmy and she put it on, feeling more like a criminal than ever.

"It's up to you, Emmy," said Victor. "You foul up and we're all done for. So don't."

Emmy didn't want to foul up, not because she was afraid of them being all 'done for', but because she wanted to stay safe and meet Emma. Nothing else mattered to her.

The garden fascinated her. She couldn't help but notice how well kept it was, the lawn neatly cut, the flower beds weeded, the shrubs pruned. She wondered what it would be like to live in such a house with such a beautiful garden, not to rob it. She moved gently along, distracted by the beauty, then saw with contempt how the three men moved with complete disinterest, heartlessly stamping down the most delicate blooms.

At the back of the house, about twelve feet up, the louver window was tightly shut.

"Don't panic," whispered Victor. "It isn't locked."

Saul stood beneath the window and cradled his hands again. He was such a big brute, Emmy thought.

She watched her father step into Saul's cradled hands. Once in position, he used a screwdriver to ease open the louver window, ever so slightly. Then he prised open the metal retaining strips and, one by one, slid out the glass slats.

Once clear, there was about thirty centimetres space. The owners might have had it in mind to secure the windows, but they hadn't thought it urgent; no one, they must have guessed, could get in through such a narrow entry.

No one except Emmy.

This was it. Emmy's crime. She hated doing it. She would have done anything not to do it, but she couldn't get away, not now.

The three men stared at her and Victor beckoned.

"Don't foul up," he whispered again. "Just do what I told you," he said, "and you'll be alright."

Emmy didn't look at him.

She stood on Saul's hands and he lifted her as if she were a feather up to the empty space. Emmy got a foothold on the window sill, grabbed the frame and made herself steady. It wasn't a long way down, but far enough to hurt herself if she fell.

She pulled herself up, squeezing her frail body into the open area, falling head first into a small bathroom, exactly what Victor told her she would find. She managed to lower herself down onto the floor without too much trouble.

She stood and looked around. Cautiously, she brought out a small torch from the pocket of her jeans and turned it on.

The bathroom was like something Emmy had

seen in picture books of palaces. Her own bathroom was rough and ready, everything chipped, broken and dirty. This was immaculate. She stared at it, knowing she should get moving, but unable to take her eyes off the gold, silver and shiny surfaces. She touched a thick towel that felt soft as silk. She thought that perhaps Victor was right, some people had everything, some had nothing, and it really wasn't fair.

"Emmy! Emmy!"

She heard her father calling from below. She looked down. The three men were staring up, impatiently. She ignored them, then turned, opened the bathroom door and peeped out.

The house was still.

In the gloom, she recognised the layout from Victor's drawings. She saw the stairs going up to the two floors and down to the cellar. She saw the doors to the bedrooms and the hallway that was supposed to lead to the front door. Everything was new and shiny and expensive. A touch of envy crept into Emmy's heart, because she saw the squalor of her own home and wondered why there should be such a difference. Was she such a bad person she had to live in her rotten little house while these people lived amidst all this newness and loveliness? It didn't make sense.

She tiptoed along the plush carpet to the street door, although the carpet was so thick she could have jumped up and down and hardly made a sound.

When she got to the door, she looked up to the left, as Victor had told her. Sure enough, hanging on a brass hook were three keys. Emmy reached up and took them.

A thought passed through her mind. She didn't

have to open the door. She could make some excuse, tell them the keys weren't there or that they didn't fit. But Victor would know, and Saul would know. Especially, her dad would know.

Reluctantly, Emmy took the largest key and slipped it into the mortise lock, turned it and heard the bolt slide open. She took the smallest and undid the chain lock. Finally, she took the medium key and slipped it into the other lock, turned it and opened the door.

"Good girl!" whispered her father.

Victor ruffled her hair.

Saul never even glanced at her, just glided in with one hand holding a torch, the other a knife.

Emmy stared at the knife in disbelief. Of course, she should have guessed Saul would carry a weapon, but it still shocked her to see a real knife, ready to hurt someone. And seeing Saul's face, she didn't doubt he wouldn't hesitate to use it, would probably even want to use it. She looked at him full in the face but he either ignored her or was preoccupied looking elsewhere. Emmy saw what she had seen before, a cold, soulless face, devoid of all kindness and compassion.

"This way," whispered Victor.

The three men knew where to go. Emmy followed them, her part in the crime almost over. She watched them go upstairs into the topmost room where Victor carefully removed a picture from a wall. Emmy had seen such things in films, but didn't think people did it for real – there was a safe in the wall.

This was where her father did what he did best. Emmy watched him with amazement as he took out a small tool box and set to work.

Emmy couldn't believe this was her father. She knew he was weak and foolish, and she knew he had served time in prison, but she still had to admire the concentration and skill he put into opening the immensely strong looking safe. She was almost proud of him, until she remembered what he was doing and where.

Saul and Victor watched and waited, their stillness making Emmy anxious. After fifteen minutes, Emmy's father whispered, "Done!" Victor patted him on the shoulder and all three men and Emmy, too, stared as Emmy's father opened the safe door.

The people that lived in the house were jewellers. They owned a company in Hatton Garden, London, where they employed half a dozen men in a cramped room to cut and polish diamonds and precious jewels. Most of the jewels were kept in a safe at the company, but they were also kept here, at the owner's home, and Victor knew that.

There were five shelves and on each shelf were stacks of smallish boxes. Victor took one out and opened it.

Emmy gaped at the beautiful necklace inside.

Something seemed to shift inside her. She doubted she would ever own such a beautiful thing, or even that she would see such a beautiful thing again. She loved it. She imagined wearing it, like the princess at a ball. She understood why her father and these greedy and dangerous men wanted it.

They opened each box in turn and each time they gazed at something more wonderful, necklaces, bracelets, rings – dozens of rings – watches, ornaments, all stunningly lovely with rubies, amethysts, emeralds and, of course, diamonds, sparkling and twinkling like starlight.

Emmy couldn't imagine how much they were worth. Thousands. Millions. She could see, just for a few moments, what made her father do what he had done, what made Saul and Victor the people they were. Emmy saw what made greedy people greedy and what made them madly jealous. These were amazing things, wonderful to behold. Emmy could have stared at them forever. She had never seen anything like them, except on television, and that was different. This was real, they were there in front of her, to be touched and felt....

Then she saw her father's face, and Victor's face, and even Saul's. Their expressions shocked her. Perhaps hers was like that, too, as if they'd seen something more important than life itself and everything else in the world had either vanished or become invisible. They all appeared hypnotised, her father as much as Victor and Saul, only there was something more dangerously intense in the features of the other two men.

Out of the madness of the moment, Emmy remembered the meeting with Emma. In a few hours they would see each other and Emmy would have to keep all this secret. She would be desperate to tell, but she mustn't. How would she be able not to tell? The jewels were the most exciting things she had ever seen! But they were still just things. They couldn't smile, they couldn't be her friend, they couldn't be anything except what they were. And most importantly, they weren't hers. They were stolen! She was helping to steal them!

Emmy felt a sudden horror at what she was doing. She hadn't had a choice, but she was still there, taking part in a serious crime.

Another side of her argued differently, that she had nothing, her father had nothing, and these people that owned this beautiful home had everything, even rare and beautiful things they kept hidden from the world. It wasn't fair and it wasn't right.

She felt ashamed of these thoughts.

"Hold the bag, Emmy!" her father whispered, giving her a tote bag to hold in which they placed a dozen or so boxes, each with a priceless piece of jewellery.

That was all they took. The house was full of electronics, books and valuable ornaments, but they only took the jewellery. Once the safe was empty, they closed it and carefully made their way downstairs.

Emmy started to breathe a little easier. She relaxed, thinking that they might very well get away with this, that she wouldn't go to prison, that no one would be hurt and that she could meet her new friend in the morning and everything would be alright. Victor had assured her that the house was empty, and it was, so once they got to the hallway on the ground floor, they had only to open the door, leave, and no one would catch them, ever.

The thought passed through her mind that, despite all her doubts, maybe these grown-ups knew better than she did and that this was not such a wrong thing to do after all. She even took off her balaclava mask which was making her hot and itchy.

That was when the street door opened and the owners stood there, suitcases in hand, looking exhausted. When they saw the four figures in their home, the look changed to one of absolute fear.

For a second everyone looked at everyone else, but the only face of the four robbers to be seen was Emmy's; all the others were still covered.

Without the balaclava Emmy could see better, and she saw Saul grip the knife. She knew what he was going to do and she couldn't let him do it.

He was going to kill the owners.

The look in his eyes was murderous and the look in the faces of the owners was one of absolute fear; they hadn't even the time or will to run away. Saul seemed to hold them in his bloodless gaze.

Emmy acted without thinking.

She took hold of Saul's hand and bit it as hard as she could, making him cry out, curse and drop the knife.

Then she ran to the owners, pushing them as hard as she could and screaming,

"Run! Run now!"

A hundred things seemed to happen at once.

The owners ran off, piercing the night with their cries for help.

Lights came on in a neighbouring house.

Saul picked up the knife and lunged at Emmy.

Emmy's father punched Saul.

Saul grabbed Emmy's father by the neck, his eyes blazing, the knife ready to strike.

Victor came between them, and with a word of command froze them both, as it they'd seen the Medusa, then he ordered them all to follow him.

Emmy's father turned and called to Emmy, "Run, Em. Run!"

"Don't you dare, you little devil," warned Victor, looking back at Emmy through the slits in the balaclava.

She wanted to run, but didn't know whether to

leave her father or stay with him. Would they hurt him if she ran? She was torn apart by indecision.

"Scarper, Emmy! Run, now, run!"

And she did, not knowing where she was going, blinded by tears, fuelled by fear, her mind in chaos, her …

15 Emma's Crime

Heart pounding, Emma boarded the train to London.

She had always done so before with her family, never alone. It had always been on a Saturday, never secretly, never with such a guilt-ridden conscience. She looked around the carriage for a spare seat, half expecting everyone to jump up, point at her and demand to know what she was doing running away from school and home when she was surrounded by so much love.

She found the last seat in a group of four, the others being taken by an elderly couple and a business woman. Emma tried not to look at any of them.

When she heard the question, she couldn't believe it was directed at her.

"Are you alright, dear?"

It was the elderly lady.

Emma tried to hide her anxiety.

"Me?"

"Yes, love," the lady said, "you look very pale. Are you alright?"

Emma cleared her throat and said, softly, that she was fine. The lady smiled and turned away, but not, Emma felt, completely. She thought she ought to change seats, but that would be rude and draw attention to herself. The best thing was to sit tight and relax. She closed her eyes, a good way of telling people around her she didn't want to talk.

Her head was buzzing and she wondered if the

lady could read her mind, or sense her anxiety. She breathed slowly and gathered her thoughts. If all went well, she would be home normal time, no one would be the wiser and she would have done a good thing, meeting The Girl who had haunted her for months. Mum and dad wouldn't know she'd been away, the school wouldn't follow up this single day's absence of their trusted star pupil, the world would just keep turning normally. It was all so easy.

Nevertheless, Emma's heart beat faster and she had to constantly fight her conscience which told her she had committed some horrendous crime.

When she opened her eyes after what seemed like an eternity, the elderly lady was looking out of the window, her husband, if it was her husband, was snoring, and the business woman was reading a paper. Nobody was taking any notice of her.

Emma shifted in her seat to get comfortable and immediately the elderly lady turned to her and smiled.

"No school today, dear?"

Emma wondered whether anyone else on the train except this one nosey woman would have taken any notice of her. It just seemed too much of a coincidence, as if fate was playing games with her. She shook her head and looked around for the toilet. It was engaged.

"You look like you've seen a ghost," said the elderly lady.

"No," Emma whispered. She opened her bag and took out a school book. She stared at it as if it was the most interesting book in the world.

The old woman turned away again, but from the corner of her eye Emma saw her occasionally turning back. Emma peered into her book, but her thoughts were elsewhere. She was wondering how she and her mysterious twin would greet each other, what they would say and how they would get on together. She had a feeling it could and would be a special friendship. There was so much Emma wanted to ask, but she wouldn't be too curious, just interested. She ...

"Good book?"

Emma looked up - the lady again, asking yet another question. Emma tried to smile, but it came out more of a grimace.

"School work," she answered, and was going to turn a page and pretend she was engrossed when the lady said,

"It's strange, you know, but it just seems a blink of an eye I was your age and going to school. Now look at me."

The lady had kind eyes, even if she was being a touch too curious. Emma guessed she didn't mean any harm, and any other time she would gladly have talked, but not now.

"Study hard," the lady went on. "I can see you're clever. How old are you? Thirteen? Fourteen?"

"Thirteen," Emma replied.

"Lovely age! I bet being old seems like something that will never ever happen. I bet you think I was born old! That's what I thought, I remember it well. Oh dear, long distant days. Are you off to school, then?"

"Yes," Emma lied.

"Isn't that a Cambridge School badge, though?"

Emma didn't know what to say. A whole bunch of lies came to mind, but none of them seemed plausible, so she just said,

"Yes," and went back to her book, but the lady persisted,

"Sorry, my dear, you're right not take any notice of me. You do your studying and I'll keep quiet."

Emma felt sorry for her, but she really didn't want to talk. Her throat was dry and she was trembling a little, especially as she'd come so close to being found out so soon. Lying wasn't easy.

At Walthamstow, she looked out of the window to see three police cars speeding down a road running parallel with the train track. Other people were also looking from the train window. The cars were heading in the same direction as the train.

"Always trouble," muttered the old lady. "People can't keep out of mischief," and she looked at Emma with a resigned expression. "Stay good," she joked.

Emma thought she was blushing, she felt so guilty. Stay good. There'd never been any doubt that she was solid gold, good from head to toe, until now. Now she felt flawed, like a precious stone with a crack through the centre, and it would never heal, it would always be visible.

The businesswoman sitting next to Emma had been quiet the whole journey, reading a newspaper and minding her own business. But now, watching the police cars, she said,

"There was a robbery last night, and an attempted murder. Two, maybe three, armed men are on the run, it says here."

The old lady tutted and said again, "Always trouble."

Emma peered out of the train window, but there was nothing to see once the police cars had gone by.

At Clapton Station, she got off the train. The elderly lady seemed surprised, as if she'd expected Emma to get off anywhere but there.

"You take care," she said.

Emma said she would.

She stood on the platform and watched the train doors slide closed and the train depart. She caught a glimpse of the elderly lady still watching her.

This was not an inviting station. There was too much grey and dark, the clocks were broken and the station buildings were shabby. A few people hovered on the opposite platform, all different to the people Emma was used to seeing near her home.

She walked up the stairs, hoping The Girl would be there, but she wasn't. Emma checked her watch, saw she was on time, and started out towards the level crossing.

The station entrance was on a main road, packed solid with buses and cars. There were shops to the left and to the right, some homes opposite. Emma felt as though she'd been transported to some distant land, it all seemed so foreign and noisy and dusty and unwelcoming. She was half tempted to take the next train back to Cambridge, but she'd come all this way and wasn't going to wimp out now.

She knew from the lay of the train lines which direction to go; she turned down the side road adjacent to the station and started walking.

The roads were narrow and busy. Cars had to pull in to allow others through in the opposite direction; people snuck in and out between them. The houses either side of the road were crammed together, all looking as though they could do with a scrub. There was something that pressed on Emma's spirit here. A police car somehow made its way down the road. Emma thought everyone was looking at her. The old woman in the train had spoken to her, the business woman had said something and now the police were following her - it was hard trying to be invisible.

About a quarter of a mile down, the road ended as it approached the river, set back behind some warehouses. On the other side of the river were the marshes and the meeting place. First, Emma had to get through the warehouses and find a route through to the river. She dared ask someone, a black lady pushing a pram, who gave her clear directions which Emma followed, and though it wasn't far, it wasn't pleasant. Emma knew she was being unforgivably foolish. This was obviously not a safe area. Gloom and secrecy hovered over the oppressive buildings like a dark cloud, and as she hurried towards the river Emma felt vulnerable. There were few people around and no one on Earth, save The Girl, knew where she was.

As soon as she emerged onto the bank of the river, her anxieties eased … a little. The river ran from left to right, and along one bank were new homes that offered a sense of security. There was a bench there and Emma sat for a moment to rest and get her bearings. Across the river spread the marshes and, slightly to the left, Emma could see the level crossing. A couple of trains passed, heading in either direction, towards or away from the centre of London. She couldn't hear them, but saw them clearly, about half a mile away, into the heart of the marshes.

There were two bridges, one far to her left, the other just a hundred yards to the right. On the other side of the river was a path where Emma thought she would be safe enough. A couple of people walked their dogs and chatted to each other. It surely couldn't be dangerous.

She thought of telephoning her parents and telling them where she was. They would be astonished, puzzled and terrified, all at the same time. But at least they would know. Emma panicked at the thought of them finding out and punishing her in some horrible way, or worse, never trusting her again. Either way, she daren't tell them. She would have to go along with her plan, see it through to the end.

She made her way towards the bridge to the right. It was an iron structure, quite old, but sound. The river at this point was just wide enough to need a bridge. Surprisingly, the atmosphere changed dramatically on the other side. Emma had a sense of freedom there, so different to the spooky streets she'd just left, and even from the opposite bank with its new homes and tidy paths.

She'd seen the marshes many times from the train window, but here they were for real, stretching into the distance with nothing to spoil the sense of wilderness and isolation.

Emma was nervous, but she was excited, too. This was the place she had stared at through the train window, and now she was seeing it from a different angle, like watching a television programme and suddenly finding yourself part of it.

Ahead and to the right lay the train line and the level crossing. It was a good distance away, and set back from the riverside path, so Emma had no option but to venture deeper into the marshes.

She checked her watch. It was almost time. She wasn't going to be late, and perhaps The Girl was early. What would they say to each other? How odd it would be to see close up that face so like her own, a face that bound them together, just as the worlds they lived in set them apart.

It took her ten minutes to reach the level crossing. At first, she had doubts. She thought it smaller than it appeared from the train. But no, it was definitely the one.

Deserted.

Not a soul in sight, just stillness and mystery for company.

The train track crossed a path rather than a road, and the path was narrower than Emma had imagined. There was also a tunnel which she assumed would be there, because she'd seen The Girl duck into it enough times, but now she could see it for herself. It, also, was smaller than she had pictured, hardly a tunnel at all, just a dark, damp, dangerous looking place beneath the railway track.

She checked her watch.

It was time, but she was still alone.

She sat for a while, wondering how long to wait. Fifteen minutes? Yes, then she would go back to the station.

It was cold in the tunnel, so she came out and stood where she could see and be seen.

Looking around, she saw very little but the stillness of East London, a park in the distance, houses beyond the river and the marshes stretching for miles. There was no sign of anyone.

Or was there?

Emma shielded her eyes from the sun to check.

Sure enough, someone was running towards her, far off, but moving quickly. Emma was impressed at how well the figure was running, balanced, controlled, swift and elegant.

It had to be…

The Girl.

And she was definitely heading for the level crossing.

Yes!

Emma breathed a sigh of relief.

But as the figure became clearer, Emma saw her repeatedly looking over her shoulder, though no one was following.

Something, however, was definitely the matter. The Girl was acting strangely, not just excited, but fraught, anxious, even terrified. Surely she couldn't be like that because she was a few minutes late?

Emma waved. The Girl didn't wave back, just kept running. Emma had a horrible fear that she might be deranged, even dangerous; after all, Emma knew nothing about her, she'd only been making up stories and they could be completely wrong.

She watched her approach, preparing to run, but The Girl was clearly afraid.

When they were within talking distance she slowed, looked over her shoulder once more, then faced Emma, flushed, anxious and holding back tears.

Time to meet.

Emma had thought about this moment for months, only now it was here, it was different. Reality was catching up with imagination.

This was not how it was supposed to be.

Something was definitely …

16   Train Ghost

"**W**rong," Emma insisted. "I saw you from the train, but I never met you."

The ghost shimmered and shook and looked pleadingly at Emma. Now that she could see the ghost's face, Emma not only saw how much alike they were, but how much concern, even desperation, there was in the ghost's features, as if it feared time was running out.

"You gotta remember," it said, "you gotta get your 'ead togever."

Emma was grateful for the ghost's concern and tried to get her head together. It was telling her not only that they'd met, but that they'd spoken, and something had happened. Wherever these memories were, Emma couldn't find them.

And yet she knew the ghost! She knew its name! As soon as the ghost had showed itself, Emma recognised it. Recognised her.

But what had happened to make it a ghost and why it was there, these were questions the ghost either couldn't or wouldn't answer.

Despite being so tired, irritable and miserable, Emma fought to fill in the blanks. Deep down she believed the ghost was right, that there was more to remember, only she didn't want to remember. The memories were not just too deeply hidden but too terrible, something told her so, and digging around for them was too dangerous.

"Fink!" the ghost said. "You don't fink, you

don't live, ain't that right? Ain't that what your dad would say?"

"I am 'finking'," Emma replied, ignoring the mystery of how the ghost knew what her dad would have said. "But we never met."

The ghost was nothing if not persistent. Emma tried to rouse herself. She felt lighter than ever, as if she could so easily drift off into dreamland. It was all too much. She wanted to see her family again, but she wanted even more just to sleep. She wished the ghost would let her be, but It wouldn't. It pestered her in a gentle, if insistent way.

"You came to see me," it said, "thas wot you did. No one else would ever 'ave done that. You came because we was gonna be friends. You bunked off school to do it."

Emma blinked. 'Bunked off school'. What a strange expression, 'bunk off'. Would she, Emma Chandler, have 'bunked off' school?

Something started to shift in Emma's memory. She held her head in her hands then looked up at the ghost.

"Did I?"

"Yeh. You did. An' it 'urt you to do it, you told me."

It would have done. A star pupil who liked school wouldn't willingly go 'bunking off'. And yet, at the same time, disconnected images and fragments of memory showed her a single, lonely journey.

She sensed a lie somewhere, knew it had meaning, didn't know how it fitted into her broken history.

The ghost was both excited and anxious. It

119

looked at the emergency stop button but didn't want to leave Emma's side.

"I'll tell you somefing about me," it said, "only it ain't good. Do you wanna know?"

"Tell me," said Emma.

The ghost was uncomfortable. It didn't like telling this story and had to force it out, word by word.

"I wos in trouble," it said. "I'd done somefing wrong. Against the law, Emma. I stole fings. I didden wanna do it, thas the troof. I was scared. I don't fink I'm bad meself. Just that … they made me … And one of 'em … one of 'em …"

"Well?"

"One of 'em was me dad."

"Your father!"

The ghost looked down.

"Yeh," it replied. "He ain't a bad man, eiver, I fink, just stupid. And I s'ppose I was stupid, too."

Emma tried to touch the ghost, to comfort it, but her hand passed through its spectral body.

"Don't suppose he was as bad as you think," said Emma reassuringly. "You're nice, so he must have been nice, too."

The ghost shook its head.

"He weren't," it said, but it looked extraordinarily grateful. It asked Emma if she really believed she - the ghost - was nice, and Emma said yes, that it had a kind heart. It must have, to be there, helping. If things weren't as they were, Emma assured her, they could be real friends.

"But thas it!" the ghost exclaimed. "Thas why you came to see me! Only it weren't at the right time. It all worked out wrong! Cos of wot I'd done. I dunno if you're gonna forgive me, Emma. Would you?"

"Forgive you?" Emma was so dreamy. The ghost's story saddened her, but she still trusted it, despite its confession. "Nothing to forgive," said Emma. "I did wrong, too, I think. We will be friends," she promised, "especially if you let me go to sleep for a while."

The ghost looked as though it could hug her to bits. It wanted forgiveness and friendship, but it needed something more, something not for itself at all, but for the sleepyhead girl who was falling away from her, second by second.

"No sleep, not now!" it exclaimed. "There ain't time. Look!"

Where the ghost was pointing, towards the end of the carriage, part of the train seemed to have vanished. Instead of clearly defined doors and seats, it was as if the blank outside world had somehow seeped in and was erasing the train, bit by bit.

"What is it?" Emma asked, rousing herself.

"The end," said the ghost, "if you don't get it togever, Emma. You gotta do it!"

Emma tried to sit up straight, to stay awake and alert.

"Do what? I don't know what I'm supposed to do!"

"Work on your 'ead," the ghost replied, "and your 'eart. Everyfing you are, you gotta get it togever! Now!"

"My 'ead?" Emma laughed, "My 'eart'? Everyfing I am … ?" she repeated, and then she cried. She felt as if she was looking into someone else's life, seeing herself 'bunk off' school, lying, cheating, running away … had she really done all that? And had she really forgotten? How could she ever forget such things? Something must have happened to make her forget, but what that was she was scared to admit.

The ghost kept talking, encouraging, asking questions. Emma, half an eye on the disappearing train, half on the stubborn ghost, answered as best she could.

She didn't know what pulled the trigger. She really felt she was just humouring the ghost more than helping.

In one fleeting, terrible moment, pieces of the jigsaw appeared and shifted and a picture emerged.

She sat up straight.

"Wot?" the ghost asked.

Emma hesitated.

"I think you're right," she whispered.

"About wot?" the ghost asked.

"About ... things ... I remember ... what did you call it, 'bunking off'. Oh, what have I done, ghost, what have I done?"

"It ain't the bunking off thas the problem, Emma," it said, "iss wot 'appened next."

It pointed to the window.

An elderly man and woman.

"They were with me, on the train," whispered Emma. "The woman kept asking me questions, questions, questions. She knew I was doing wrong."

"You didden do wrong," the ghost said. "No more'n me, less'n me. Come on, Emma. look. Remember!"

Emma fought the tiredness, but there were pains in her body, too, though she didn't know from what. The ghost saw her squirm and said,

"Wassa matter?"

"Bits of me hurt," Emma whispered.

The ghost's eyes shone – it would have cried if it could.

"It'll be alright," it whispered, urgently. "It's gotta be!"

Emma tried to smile at the ghost but she found it hard. Her face hurt and her body hurt and she really didn't want to talk or do anything except close her eyes, but the ghost's concern kept her mind busy.

All the while, the blank outside world that had seeped in was now eating the train carriage, inch by inch. Both Emma and the ghost watched it, terrified. Bits of the door vanished. Then the whole door had gone. Some seats disappeared, too.

"Move!" the ghost ordered. "We gotta get to the uvver end of the carriage."

She persuaded Emma to stand, which Emma did with lots of grumbles and pains, and they stumbled down to the far end of the train, near the emergency stop button.

"You're not doing this on purpose, are you ghost?" Emma asked, "just to get me to press the button?"

"I ain't doing nuffing," the ghost said. "You gotta do it all yourself, Emma. If that … that … nuffingness stuff gets us, we're in trouble!"

The 'nuffingness stuff' was eating the train, row by row.

"What is it?" Emma asked, still trying to use logic and her once sharp mind to work out what was happening.

"Dunno for sure," the ghost answered, "but do you wanna be gobbled up by it?"

Emma didn't, but neither did she know how to stop it. The nothingness was heading their way.

They were at the end of the carriage close to the doors. Above them was the red button, still and silent. Emma stared at it, stared at the oncoming 'nuffingness', and stared at the ghost which was looking at her with tears in its eyes.

"You care about me, don't you?" Emma asked, quizzically. "That's why you're crying."

"I do!" the ghost answered, full of affection. "You're me friend!"

Memories flooded in.

Emma saw herself on the marshes.

She saw herself waiting to meet The Girl.

She saw the figure running towards her.

She remembered thinking that something was wrong.

She remembered The Girl, frightened to death, crying out ...

17 First Meetings

" . . . I didden know wot to do! I didden know where to go! It is you, innit?"

Emma, uncertain herself, tried to reassure The Girl, who was clearly distressed.

"It's me. Emma. I came to meet you, like you asked."

The Girl looked over her shoulder.

"We gotta hide," she said, "then I'll tell you everyfing."

She led Emma down the bank under the level crossing. They sat on the stone ledge and The Girl squeezed Emma's hand. They studied each other, fascinated.

"It weren't supposed to be like this," said The Girl, "Honest."

"Be like what?" Emma asked.

"Dangerous," said The Girl, looking to either side of the tunnel, anxiously.

Emma's heart beat a little faster. Dangerous? What was happening?

"Tell me your name first," she said, "then tell me why it's dangerous."

"You won't believe me."

Emma couldn't think why.

"Try me," she said.

"I know your name," The Girl said. "You wrote it on the note. You're Emma."

"That's right."

"And I'm Emmy. True. Thas my name. Emmy."

Emma, delighted, said, "Emmy! Emmy! How strange!"

"Tis, innit," said Emmy. "I ain't making it up. It's like yours, only not exact. Just like me and you, we're not exact neiver."

"No," Emma agreed, "but it's awfully close."

Despite her evident anxiety, Emmy smiled. Yes, they were incredibly alike. Any differences were more because of the lives they led than real physical differences, Emmy being thinner and paler, but otherwise they might truly have been identical twins.

"'Emmy'," whispered Emma. "I can't believe it!"

Emmy kept a tight grip on Emma's hand.

"You won't hate me, will ya," she asked, "when I tell you wos 'appened?"

Emma put her other hand on the frightened girl's trembling fingers.

"Hate you? Don't say such a thing! I'm your friend, or I want to be, if you'll let me," said Emma. "Like twins, that's what we are, and twins are friends for ever."

Emmy looked up, her eyes shining.

"You say that cos you don't know me," she said. "I gotta tell you somefing. Somefing bad."

Emma wondered what badness this frail, unhappy girl could reveal, but doubted it was anything truly terrible, and even if it was, she wouldn't back away.

Emmy took a deep breath and started her story.

"Last night," she said, "I did somefing. I didden wanna do it, but I didden have a choice. Me dad and his

126

friends, they made me. Me dad's a baddun," said Emmy. "Not always. Sometimes I like 'im, sometimes. He's funny sometimes, and when I wos a little girl he was alright, but fings went wrong, wiv 'im and mum, and she left, and ee's been in prison a bit and thas where 'e met Saul and Victor."

Emma tried to keep calm. Prison! Prison was something she heard about on the news, not knew about in real life. What was her new friend going to tell her?

"They're the ones I'm runnin' from," said Emmy. "Saul and Victor. They're bad men and I didden mean to get you mixed up wiv 'em."

"But I'm not mixed up with them," Emma said. "I've never seen them."

"Thas right," Emmy continued. "An I don't want you to see 'em. If they find us 'ere, we're in trouble."

Emma was trying to piece together the story, but Emmy was so upset she wasn't telling it properly.

"Tell me what happened last night," Emma said, "from the beginning."

Emmy was quiet for a few seconds, gathering her thoughts. She kept looking to the left and right, making sure the coast was clear.

"They made me do a burgle," she said.

"A what?"

"A burgle. We burgled an 'ouse. They made me break into an 'ouse and open the door so's they could get in and they did, and they stole stuff and we would've got away but the owners they came back early and caught us."

Emma stared. What was this? She'd trusted The Girl when she was The Girl, but now she had a name, Emmy, and a life, things were real, not imaginary, and disturbing. The only thing that gave her strength was the belief that Emmy was solid gold, despite the story she was telling, and Emma desperately wanted to help. Nevertheless, she was shaken.

"You broke into a house?" Emma asked. "Someone else's house?"

Emmy nodded.

"Told you it was bad," she said. "I wish I ain't done it, but I did it. They made me. They would've 'urt me, Emma. You'd know what I mean if you saw them, not me dad, but the uvvers, specially Saul. He's a tall bloke, really tall, and he ain't got nuffing inside."

"Nothing inside?"

"No. He's empty, like a robot. He 'urts people. He 'urt my dad."

"But I thought they were friends."

"They were. They are. But … well…they ain't normal."

"Tell me everything," said Emma.

Emmy told her how Saul, Victor and her father had been planning, how they'd forced her to help, how they'd got into the house and how it had all seemed to be going easily when the owners came back.

"I bit 'im," said Emmy. "I bit Saul. On the 'and."

"You bit him! Why?"

"Cos he was gonna kill 'em. He 'ad a knife and he was gonna kill 'em."

"So you bit his hand? Emmy, that was brave!"

"It was stupid. He turned on me. He would've killed me, I fink, but me dad 'it im."

Emma felt as though she was hearing about a television soap opera rather than real life. It was as if a whole new and not so wonderful world had opened up before her, and she was afraid of it.

"What happened next?" she asked Emmy.

"I ran. I didden wanna, because I fought they'd 'urt me dad if I did. But he told me to, he yelled at me to run, and I did, I ran and ran and I've been runnin' froo the night. Runnin' an' 'idin'. I dunno what they've done wiv me dad. I 'ope they 'aven't hurt him, Emma. I'm so mixed up and tired!"

Emma put her arm around Emmy's shoulders. She could feel the girl trembling with fear and exhaustion. She stroked Emmy's hand, trying to calm her down, but she was anxious herself now, so close to such terrible things.

"You must be fast to run away from men," she said.

"I am," Emmy replied, "I can run better'n anyone." Emma saw that their similarities weren't just skin deep. "And you might 'ave to run fast, too, if they find us. I didden wanna come 'ere, cos they're gonna try and find me. But I knew you were comin', so I 'ad to tell you, to warn you."

Emma hadn't imagined their first meeting would be like this, not in a thousand years. She half wished she hadn't come, that she had listened to her inner voice and conscience, but another inner voice and conscience had told her to meet The Girl, and it still said she had done the right thing.

Right or wrong, this wasn't playacting any more, this was real, and it meant she was in danger, they were both in danger.

"To warn me?"

"In case they find us! Supposing you'd come and I weren't 'ere and they'd found you and got you and you lookin' like me 'an all. I dunno, Somefing might 'ave 'appened to you. I 'ad to come, Emma."

This was a whole new world Emma had stepped into, and she hadn't just stepped into it, she had jumped into it, exposed and vulnerable. There she was, sitting in a tiny tunnel with a girl she hardly knew, drawn in to crime and murder and imminent threat.

She stood up.

"I'm going to take you home with me," she said, firmly. "My mother and father will know what to do. I can't leave you here."

Emmy looked astonished.

"You'd do that?" she asked. "I fort you'd 'ate me. I 'ate meself."

"I don't hate you," said Emma. "This isn't your fault, not if you've told me the truth."

"I 'ave. S'all true. Every word. I wish it weren't, but it is."

Emma took Emmy's hand again and held it tightly.

"I'm lucky," she said, "I've got a good mum and dad, I go to a good school, I can do anything I want, almost. I can help you. Will you let me?"

Emmy stood up, too, her heart pounding through tiredness and fear. She said, "I don't want you feelin' sorry for me. I jus' want you t' like me."

Emma hugged her new and troubled friend.

"I do feel sorry for you," she said. "I can't help it. But I like you a lot."

Emmy laughed. It was so unexpected a thing for her to do, her face creased and her eyes sparkled, just for a few moments.

"You fink so?"

"I know so. Look, we better not stay here. Do these people, Saul and Victor, know about this place?"

Emmy wasn't sure.

"Me dad might have told 'em," she said.

"Then we're not safe," said Emma. "We'll get back to the station, take the first train to Cambridge."

"Cambridge, eh? What you gonna do in Cambridge, then, Em?"

Both girls turned.

At one end of the tunnel stood a short, stocky, tough looking man, half smiling, half gloating.

Victor.

"What d'you want to run away from?.... Stone me!"

Victor had suddenly realised he was looking at two Emmys. His eyes darted from girl to girl.

"You leave 'er alone!" Emmy screamed. "You don't touch 'er! She ain't got nuffing to do wiv you!"

"She has now, whoever she is," said Victor, softly.

Emmy grabbed Emma's hand.

"It's Victor!" she said. "Run, Emma. Run! Just follow me!"

Emmy pushed Emma towards the other end of the tunnel, just as Saul appeared.

Emmy slipped past Saul but Saul grabbed Emma and stared at her.

"Who the ...?"

"My name is Emma!" said Emma, terrified, but determined not to show her fear. "Now let me go!"

Saul almost did let her go, he was so surprised to see this replica of Emmy, yet clearly not Emmy. Then Victor called out,

"Hold her!"

And he clamped his arm around her mouth.

Emmy was about twenty yards away. She stopped running.

"Let her go! Let her go! She ain't nuffing to do wiv me. I just met 'er."

Victor climbed out and up and smiled at Emmy.

"Of course I'll let her go. Don't know her, don't want to know her, though I have to say, Emmy, she's an awful lot like you and that's a mysterious thing. But before I let her go, you have to come back. We need you, Emmy."

Emmy was furious, more with herself than the two hateful men.

"Let her go then," she said, "an I'll come back. I promise."

Victor laughed.

"Now, now. I'm not that foolish. You come back here and we'll let her go. Emma is it? Curiouser and curiouser. Come on Emmy."

Emmy seethed inside. They'd been so close to getting away. A few seconds, that was all! Another few seconds and they'd have got clean away, back to the station, back to Emma's home and safety. Now it had all gone wrong.

She walked back, slowly, staring at Saul.

"Don't hurt her, you rotten, stinkin' pig!"

Saul laughed and tightened his grip on Emma.

"In the car," Victor ordered Emmy who had half expected him to hit her.

"Well," said Emmy, when they reached the car, "Let 'er go."

"Can't do that," said Victor. "Sorry."

Emmy screamed,

"Let 'er go! Let 'er go! Let…"

Victor smacked her across the face and a little blood dribbled from her mouth.

"You see," Victor said. "We might not know who she is, but she knows us now, our names and faces and all. So we're hardly going to let her go running off into the wild blue yonder, are we? This is all your fault, Emmy, you know that. If you hadn't interfered last night, bit poor old Saul's hand, we might not be in this position."

Emmy cursed and scratched like a mad thing, though she cared nothing for what they might do to her any more, only for Emma who sat white with fear in the back seat besides a silent, menacing Saul.

Victor was far too strong, and eventually bundled Emmy into the front seat, his eyes red with anger, his hand bleeding from her scratches. He sat in the driving seat but didn't drive off straight away, holding her down and tying her hands and feet. Saul felt no need to tie the quiet girl beside him.

"Can't have a super athlete like you running loose can we?" joked Victor, regaining his composure.

He looked over his shoulder and asked politely,

"So you're Emma?"

"Don't you do nuffing to 'er!" screamed Emmy.

Saul was going to hit her but Victor stopped him.

"Look," he whispered, comfortingly, to both girls. "You know what they say on television programs when the criminals are caught…?"

"We ain't criminals!"

"Right. Well, you are Em. Don't know about

your twin sister here. They say we can either play this by the book or you make it hard on yourselves. Something like that. You get the gist, though?"

Emma sat perfectly still. She listened to Victor's snakelike voice and looked into Saul's cruel eyes. She couldn't believe this had happened. It was a nightmare beyond nightmares. All she wanted was to pretend it wasn't happening, to go back a day, a few hours, just go back and change things. How had she ended up here, on the back seat of a car with two such men as this threatening her?

"Emma," she whispered, "My name is Emma."

Victor laughed. Even Saul smiled.

"Weird or what?" observed Victor. "Well, we haven't time to find out the history of this weird or what meeting. Suffice to say, Emma, and you look bright enough to know what's happening, this isn't good. Nevertheless, you'll be alright if you behave and don't go biting or scratching like this little demon here."

Emmy said nothing, just trembled with fury. She turned, surprised, when she heard Emma ask, quietly and calmly,

"What are you going to do with us?"

Emmy registered the question. 'Us'. Not 'me'. 'Us'.

Victor hesitated.

"I imagine Emmy has told you what happened. The problem is that our runaway here showed her little face last night and that was foolish. We could have and should have sorted the problem there and then, but she rather did for all of us, bit the hand that fed her, you might say."

"I bit HIS hand," said Emmy. "He never fed me

nuffing."

"Figure of speech, Emmy. So, we have limited time. The police will find out about Emmy, about her father and about us. Pretty soon, I'd say. Meanwhile, we have a few hundred thousand pounds worth of jewels to fence – to sell, that is – ASAP, and to leave the country. So we can't waste time. You two get locked away safely for a while, we get our money and disappear. End. What do you think, Emma?"

Emma thought she should just sit still and hope Victor meant what he said. But at the same time she felt the atmosphere still threatening, especially with Saul so close to her.

"I won't say anything," she answered. "Nor will Emmy. Let us go."

Again 'us', not 'me'. Emmy thought her heart would break. Emma had risked all kinds of things just to meet worthless, useless Emmy, and what had Emmy done, only what she always did, make a mess, lead her new friend into this horror. She hated herself more than ever.

Victor laughed.

"I'd like to," he answered. "But I can't. We're in a bit of bother here and, if we let you go, that bother will get worse."

"It won't," Emma whispered, so scared that her voice was hardly heard. "We won't say a thing."

Victor's smile disappeared.

"We know you won't," he said.

And he started the car.

The track was rough, not meant for regular traffic. Victor had taken a big chance driving onto it, because it made them conspicuous, but there was no one around, not that time on a Monday morning.

He drove slowly, heading towards the Marina where the track merged with a proper road. Both girls were quiet. They'd been warned, if they screamed or drew attention, they would be hurt, and Saul looked ready to carry out the threat.

Emma sat silent, still disbelieving, wishing herself home. She had never been so scared in her life, never thought she could be so scared, nor imagined she ever would be again. All kinds of scenarios passed through her mind and she tried to fight them off, to stay calm. She looked at Emmy sitting in the front seat, desperately unhappy, visibly trembling with fear and fury. She felt only pity, no anger. She didn't know exactly what had happened, but she saw now how devastatingly unfair life could be and knew this wasn't Emmy's fault. She wanted to help, to turn Emmy's life around, and would, if she ever had the chance.

Which was doubtful.

She thought that she was going to die and was terrified. She didn't understand what it meant or why it was going to happen. Her life was perfect, so full of lovely people, lovely things. She had so much going for her, but now it was all going to be taken away in the most horrid of ways. How would her family deal with it? Would they blame her for running away like the stupid, foolish girl she was?

She pushed the thought aside and tried to think if there was anything at all she could do. But as hard as she thought, no answer came. If this was television, something would happen to save her. But there was no hope here in an unforgiving reality. Saul sat beside her like some still, silent marble faced death. She had never thought such people existed, pure cruelty. She wondered how he and her father could both be human and live on the same planet. But they did, and he, Saul, was there, barely a few inches away from her, his presence filling her with fear.

The car reached the marina and edged onto a gravelled road. There were more people around and the thought occurred to Emma to take a chance, just make one loud, fearful scream. But she knew it wouldn't work. The window was closed, the people wouldn't hear and before the scream left her mouth the monster Saul would be on her. She shivered and closed her eyes.

They reached the junction with a main road. The contrast was striking, from the peace and tranquillity of the marshes to the sudden onrush of cars, flying by in both directions.

Victor stopped the car and waited for a space to join the flow of traffic.

It was odd, Emma thought, that there were now thousands of people around, and they would all help, if only they knew! But they didn't know. Emma felt more alone and hopeless so close to the world again than she had a few moments before in the wilderness of the marshes. She thought of her parents, Cal, Benjy, her friends and teachers and tried to send her thoughts to them, hoping that somehow they might receive these mental messages of distress.

The car moved forward, turning right across the flow of traffic.

Emma saw Emmy move, but the movement was lightning fast and took her by surprise. Emmy had been sitting still as stone for minutes, not speaking, not crying, not a whimper. As the car eased into the fast moving line of cars, Emmy leaned over and, with a face of pure hatred, bit deep into Victor's left hand. Victor swore aloud and turned on Emmy with eyes aflame, brought his right hand away from the steering wheel and smacked her across the head.

The car veered.

Saul leaned forward with stunning speed to grab the wheel and steady the car.

But it was too late.

Emma had time to see and hear the world turn upside down. There was colour and movement everywhere, as if a rainbow of metal had engulfed them. For a split second it was quiet, the lull before the storm. Then there was an unholy noise as if the world had become unhinged and toppled on top of them. She felt as if there would never be anything else but that sound of twisting metal, flying glass and crumpling bodies.

Thankfully, it simply stopped, instantaneously, all the mayhem, the thunderous crashes and the horrible pain of collisions.

All of it vanished.

And then…

If she had been asleep, it had been the strangest of sleeps, and if she was now awake, it was the strangest of ….

18   Trauma

"Waking can be a long and difficult process," said the consultant. "or it can be sudden. We don't really know what's going on in her mind, you see."

They were sitting in a small, private ward of a large London hospital. Around the bed were Mr. and Mrs. Chandler, Benjy on Mrs. Chandler's lap, Calum at the foot of the bed and Emmy, sitting still as stone, a bandage supporting a broken left arm, her right hand firmly holding Emma's hand.

Emmy was the only one to whom Emma responded. It was something which Emma's family didn't understand, but there was no denying, she returned to the world when Emmy was present, fell away when Emmy left.

The accident had killed Saul, done nothing to Victor, broken Emmy's arm but left Emma in a coma. That had been three weeks ago. Once the family had been notified, they had come to London and never left. They had also met Emmy Fairchild and were unable to explain her place in their daughter's life.

"It was my fault," Emmy said, in the beginning, "but I'll make her better, honest. I will."

Gradually, Emmy's story was made known. The police were called, the social services, too. Mr. Fairchild, who had been beaten by his two 'friends', confessed. Victor didn't. He just smiled and joked as if nothing much had happened and nothing much mattered.

"The girl alright, then?" he asked, as if Emma had a slight cold. This was as much as he could offer.

Mr. and Mrs. Chandler had disturbingly mixed feelings towards Emmy. They couldn't help but lay part of the blame for the accident on her, though they never said this to her face, just thought it. They couldn't understand how their daughter, normally so good and trustworthy, had been led to do such a thing as truant and meet with this strange young girl. Despite the striking resemblance, no one could be more different from their beloved Emma than this poor, solitary creature, so frail and so full of frustrated love. If the consultant hadn't suggested it, they wouldn't have wanted her in the ward with Emma, but Emma showed distinct signs of awareness and consciousness when she was there.

"In previous cases," the consultant went on, "where the patient has come out of such a coma, they told of focusing on one particular idea, as if they had to be fixed on something, obsessively, that would lead them out of their comatose state. That might be happening here. It could be, but we really don't know for sure, that Emmy has somehow focused your daughter's mind on – I don't know – an image, an object, an idea – it could be anything, but certainly Emmy and Emma have some peculiar and strong bond. They are amazingly alike, of course, and must have made some connection to arrange that meeting, one which has deeply affected your daughter and which, I believe, is keeping her alive in some way. She's been through a terrible trauma and it's a wonder she's still with us."

It was a wonder. The back of the car was hit by a

transit van and, considering that Saul perished, it was miraculous that Emma survived. She fought hard and was never left to fight alone. At one time of the day or another, someone was in the room with her. Emmy would never have left if she had her way. The only time she did was when she fell asleep and the staff took her to a visitor's room.

No one knew yet what to do with Emmy. Her father was clearly incapable of raising her properly and her mother hadn't been traced yet. All Emmy wanted to do, all she insisted on doing, was staying in the ward, keeping watch and holding Emma's hand whenever Emma's parents allowed it. There were moves to take her into care, but they all felt it wasn't time yet, and that she was serving some important if inexplicable purpose there by Emma's side.

Emmy herself said little, but looked at Mr. and Mrs. Chandler with such sadness and sorrow. She hated herself more than ever, for what she thought she had done, and for surviving the crash, but she lay her anger aside, focusing all attention on her injured friend. She talked to Emma and never let her thoughts drift from praying – to nothing in particular – that Emma should hear her and open her eyes.

To do this, she made up a story.

She pretended that Emma was in a train and that, to get better, she had to stop it moving. If she didn't, it would take her to heaven and Emma would be gone from the world. Emmy whispered the story, more to herself than to her friend, over and over, quietly, insistently, endlessly. It was a nice, easy idea. Trains were their common bond, and here was a train taking Emma, like an angel, to heaven, only Emma wasn't ready yet for heaven. You could sleep in heaven and you wouldn't be disturbed, ever, but there was a time for all things and this wasn't Emma's time.

When she didn't speak it, Emmy thought it, and sent it almost like an electric signal along her arm and her hand into Emmy's limp body.

If there had been any indication that Emmy was doing their daughter harm, Mr. and Mrs. Chandler would have sent her away without hesitation or compassion, but the doctors said otherwise, and though they didn't understand, they let things be and waited.

And waited.

Days passed and Emma lay in her coma, unspeaking, unseeing, but perhaps not unhearing. There was an almost holy quiet in the room, not simply the quiet of hushed tones, but of something deeper and more mysterious. Emma's spirit could be felt, even heard, struggling to return. Her breathing was different, slower and more regular, carrying with it all her deep strength and energy. Though the room was quiet, it was charged to the full with frantic hopes and unmentionable fears. Only the staff and family came into the room, a room hung with countless cards from all over the country and all over the world. The cards had been strung across the walls, each one with the loveliest wishes from those who had heard and wondered at the story.

It was, by then, major news. It was unique and had captured hearts and minds. As unwilling as the family was to share anything of what had happened with the outside world, the story hit the media and the media watched and people hoped. Mr. and Mrs. Chandler never said a word. They were left alone, as they wanted to be, and all that was passed to the media were brief bulletins by the doctor.

The priority, of course, was Emma, and her critical condition. People prayed if they were religious, hoped and sent her their love if they weren't. Places of worship said special prayers, but the greatest stream of energy came from the millions of people with compassion in their hearts and a wish for life to resolve positively this inexplicable sadness.

The hospital room, decked out with cards, was the focal point of good will from countless people, all of whom wanted Emma to recover - it was filled and fuelled by their love.

Only Emmy was unaware of it. To her, the outside world didn't exist. The only thing that mattered was her friend and their peculiarly brief but significant history. As much as the world was wishing Emma well, and as much as her family devoted all their energy to her recovery, Emmy still had the more powerful bond to the injured girl. No one understood why, but the responses on the charts proved it.

"I'll take over now," said Emma's mother after Emmy had been sitting holding Emma's hand for an hour. Emmy never argued or pleaded. Even if she desperately wanted to stay and keep holding Emma's hand, she always did exactly what the family asked. She believed, with some foundation, that Emma's family blamed her for leading their daughter into this disaster. She let go Emma's hand and went to sit in the corner and waited.

"Don't you want anything to eat, Emmy?" asked Mrs. Chandler.

She shook her head and said,

"No fanks."

"Something to drink?"

"No fanks."

Mrs. Chandler turned to her daughter, sat and held her hand. Emmy watched Emma's mother and felt unbearably sad. She could see how much the family loved Emma and she kept telling herself it was her fault they were suffering so much. She felt unwanted, the cause of the unhappiness, and that she was in their way, even now, especially now. She thought everyone would be relieved if she wasn't there at all, but she couldn't go, she just couldn't. She knew she was getting through to Emma, she felt it with all her heart, and if she left she dreaded what might happen.

"Are you alright, Emmy?"

This was Cal, Emma's brother. He came to sit next to her and put his hand on her shoulder. "You look a bit tired."

"I'm alright. Fanks."

Cal smiled. He had a tender smile and Emmy liked him. He seemed friendly and she didn't get the mixed up vibes she got from Mr. and Mrs. Chandler. Cal was fascinated by Emmy, how similar she was to his sister and how hard she was trying to make Emma well again.

"Let's go outside for a while. You need something to eat and drink. So do I. Come on."

He took her to the canteen where Emmy, unexpectedly, felt suddenly really proud to have Cal treat her and talk to her.

"What are you thinking about?" Cal asked, once they'd found a table.

"Nuffing much. Dunno what to fink."

Cal smiled.

"None of us do. We don't blame you, you know."

Emmy looked at him. She wished she could believe him, and perhaps he was speaking the truth for himself, but she didn't think it was the truth for his mum and dad. Her eyes filled with tears but she refused to cry.

"I didden mean to do nuffing," she said. "Somefing made us like each uvver. Thas all."

"We all need friends, Emmy. I think Emma's lucky she's got you."

Emmy looked up at Cal as if he'd said the best thing it was possible to say.

"D'you mean it?" she asked.

Emmy's heart was full to bursting. It meant everything for Cal to like her.

"You have to understand," said Cal, "they don't hate you, Emmy. "They haven't much space in their hearts for anything else except Emma. When she's better they'll talk to you more."

"Don't matter," said Emmy. "The only fing that ma'ers is she gets be'er."

Cal asked her questions about her life and was intrigued by her hardships and struggles. He could see how much was locked away, and was wise enough, even at his age, to see there was a much brighter and happier person hidden inside. He decided, if Emma got better – when Emma got better - he'd help. And his mum and dad would help, too, he would make them.

Later that day, Emma's father sat with her in the ward. Emmy flinched for a moment in case he was going to tell her to leave, that they didn't want her there any more.

"We haven't talked to you much," he said.

"Sorry, Emmy."

Emmy stared at him, bewildered. Emma's father, of all people, had apologised to her. No one ever did that. Not for anything.

"S'alright," she said.

"Cal told me he talked to you. He likes you. We all do, Emmy. Don't think otherwise."

Whatever blame attached to this tragedy, Emmy was innocent of it, he knew that, despite lingering, less generous thoughts which he laid aside.

"Fanks," she answered.

Mr. Chandler looked at Emmy and said,

"It's amazing. Close up, you're more alike than ever. You really could be her twin."

"I know," said Emmy. "Thas why we wanted to meet. I didden know this would 'appen. Honest."

"Of course you didn't," said Mr. Chandler. "No one thinks you did. To be honest, we're all amazed you're such a good girl, considering, well…"

"You mean me dad an 'all?"

"I suppose so. And his friends."

"They weren't really his friends," said Emmy. "Friends is what does nice fings for you and loves you more than anyfing in the world. They weren't like that, Saul and Victor, they were juss people he knew in … in …"

"Prison?"

"Yeh. They was rubbish people."

Mr. Chandler put his arm around her.

"We'll bring her back," he said.

They let her be with Benjy. First time, Benjy stared at Emmy in wonder.

"You're not Emma," he said.

"No I ain't."

"No, I'm not," Benjy corrected.

"No, I'm not," said Emmy.

At first, Benjy didn't know what to make of this mirror image of his sister. He hovered around her a lot, stared at her, but said little. Then, once he got used to her, he waited by her side and wanted to be with her wherever she went.

"Is Emma going to die?" he asked her.

"No!" said Emmy. "She ain't! You mustn't fink it."

"Why's she lying down so much, then?"

"Because she's hurt. She needs to sleep."

"But she's not waking up."

"She will," said Emmy. "I'll make her. We'll make her."

Benjy didn't understand. It looked so simple, Emma was asleep, well, wake her up. What was so hard about that?

It was Mrs. Chandler who found it hardest to talk with Emmy. As good hearted as the girl was, she was the one who had invited Emma to play truant. She had to take some blame. Mrs. Chandler tried to overcome her anger, and she did, once she'd learned the full story, or at least as much of the story as the police could tell her. Nevertheless, a residue of irritation remained. If it wasn't for this odd girl, Emma would be with them, alive and well, and life would have been going on normally. If Mrs. Chandler was honest with herself, she had, at first, hated Emmy. She thought Emmy crude and foolish and blamed her entirely for the accident. But as the days passed she found ways to deal with her anger and began to see the charm of the girl and her total dedication to Emma's recovery. She also saw how regret was eating up Emmy, like a monster gnawing away inside her, but even then Mrs. Chandler could not dispel her ill feelings. It was only when the doctors told her that Emmy's time with Emma seemed to bring such a good response did she start looking at her in a new light, even if it was with a touch of jealousy. After a couple of weeks, she talked to her more often and began to see all the good things inside - innocence, kindness, determination and joy. She wondered what would happen to her after … well, just after.

But of course her sole concern was Emma. Mrs. Chandler felt as though she was balanced on a tightrope high in the sky, and that if Emma died she would fall and fall and continue to fall forever. She loved her daughter so much, life without her would be no life at all. She never gave moment to thoughts of absence, just of recovery. When she held Emma's hand, she squeezed it gently and talked to her constantly, rubbing the fingers, trying to sense some movement and response.

All the time, Emma lay like marble.

"What do you say to her, Emmy?" Mrs. Chandler asked, one afternoon.

"Just talk to her," said Emmy, "like what you do."

"The doctor says you've made up a story to tell her. What is it?"

Emmy shrugged.

"Nuffing much. Iss private. I'm trying to make 'er do somefing."

"Do what?"

"Listen to me, thas all. Listen to all of us. Get better. Ain't nuffing special."

"She seems to need you," said Mrs. Chandler.

"Cos I was there when it 'appened," said Emmy. "I dunno why else, 'cept cos of the way we look. I fink she feels sorry for me, too."

Mrs. Chandler heard the earnestness in Emmy's voice and found it hard to dislike her. She was a good girl in a bad world.

Weeks passed. The Chandler family got to know Emmy and saw how serious she was, how untiring and how true a heart she had. They couldn't hold any grudges when they saw she would willingly have given her own life for Emma's.

Every time Emmy looked at Emma, she cried inside. She wanted to cry on the outside, too, but she daren't. She needed every ounce of energy and determination to help Emma, and she knew she was helping. She felt it so strongly, but she had to get Emma to trust her. How could she, as they'd only met for less than an hour? She had no idea what was going on in Emma's mind, but she just kept telling her to listen, trust her and get better.

Sometimes Emma drifted away. Her breathing and body rhythm slowed. They all panicked then, thinking she was falling and wouldn't be able to pull herself up again, but she did, every time. Emmy sensed the moments they were losing Emma and also the moments when she roused herself.

"You gotta listen to me," she whispered. "You gotta do what I tell you. You gotta wake up, Emma. S'no good goin' to sleep. You don't wanna sleep now. You wanna move yourself, do somefing, whatever you're finking of, just do it. No good doin' nuffing. If you give up, I'm gonna blame meself forever till I die.

You don't wanna do that to me, do you? Course you don't. It ain't fair. It ain't right. They all love you, your mum and dad and Calum and Benjy. You should see them, Emma, I wish I 'ad a family like that! There's no way you're gonna let them go. They ain't gonna live wivout you, neiver am I. You gotta get back, you gotta fight. You're a good racer like me, they told me that, so we gotta race each uvver, iniit? Cal told me you always win. He said you're the best. Well, you gotta get better an' race me, thas what you gotta do. Fink of your mum and dad and all of 'em. Fink of runnin', fink of racing me, cos we will. I'm good, too. Iss the only fing I'm good at, runnin'. I never get tired, not when I run, not never, and I won't get tired talkin' to you now. I'll keep on even if I get on your nerves, because if I leave you you're gonna go to sleep and thas no good, no good at all. So do it, do whatever it is in your 'ead you 'ave to do and come back. You can't let us down, Emma, you can't. I'd shout at you, but I mustn't. They'd chuck me out. No, I gotta talk quietly, we all gotta talk quietly, thas what the doctor says, but I fink we should shout. Wassa point of whisperin' if we wanna wake you? Daft, innit. But I'm doin' what I'm told and you gotta do what you're told. Iss been ages you lyin' 'ere. Iss time to get up. Right? Time to stop all this sleepin'. I know you can 'ear me, so listen, becoz I'm your best friend ever, and who you gonna trust if you can't trust ya best friend? Come back, Emma. Trust me and come back. All you gotta do is ..."

19   Ghost Train

"Trust me!" the ghost urged Emma, "I dunno why you don't!"

"I do," Emma replied, sleepily. "You're my friend."

"Always will be," said the ghost, with great affection. "You got loads o' friends that love you. Remember them. Now look, and do somefing!"

Most of the carriage had disappeared, vanished into the nothingness that was closing in, a noose of oblivion.

"Doesn't scare me," said Emma. "It's quite peaceful."

"No! It ain't peaceful!" exclaimed the ghost. "Peaceful's rubbish. Iss a lie, iss gonna rub you out, Emma. Remember again! Go on, you said you did!"

Emma knew what the ghost meant now, the marshes, the meeting, The Girl, the men, the car, the fear – but so what, it was just a memory. It meant nothing. That was why the nothingness was closing in on her, because the nothingness was really truth and peace, freedom from pain, freedom to sleep forever.

"I do remember," she said to the ghost, "You were there, weren't you? I came to meet you."

"Thas right. You did! An' then everyfing went wrong."

"Yes, it did, didn't it. But what happened then? Will you tell me?"

The ghost twitched and cried and seemed reluctant to say what it had to say.

"You ain't gonna like it."

"Tell me anyway, my little ghost friend."

The ghost appeared to move up and down, ever so slightly, ever so slowly, as if it were breathing, and Emma felt she could rise and fall in the same way, she was so light and airy herself now.

"Thas the fing," said the ghost.

"What is? What's the thing?"

"Wot you called me."

"I didn't call you anything. You're just a ghost. Ghosts don't have names."

The ghost trembled in despair.

"Silly, silly girl!" it exclaimed. "Don't you understand yet? I ain't the ghost! You are!"

Emma looked at the ghost's face and at last she understood. She felt terribly sad because she feared she'd understood too late. She knew what had happened, not all of it, but enough.

"Am I?" she said. "How funny! And all the time I thought it was you!"

"It ain't funny!" the ghost-girl called Emmy answered. "Iss serious. You gotta get yourself togever. There ain't time to muck around no more."

Emma didn't feel that she was mucking around. She tried to think clearly, although she spoke ever more slowly and listlessly.

"If that's true," she said, "and I'm the ghost, which sounds silly, but let's say it's true, how come I can touch things and you can't? Answer me that, ghost-girl."

"My ... name ... is ... Emmy," said the ghost-girl, with a long sigh.

"Emmy," whispered Emma, very softly. "Nice

name. My name was like that. What was it?"

"Your name is Emma. Not was. Is!"

"Right. Well, Emmy, answer the question. How come I can touch things and you can't?"

Emmy thought.

"Because you belong here, I don't. You're a ghost and this is a ghost train. Don't you get it?"

The real ghost felt like weeping. The emptiness looked so comforting, so peaceful, and all it wanted to do was be at peace, because it still hurt, and it was more tired than all the tired people in all the world put together. Then it looked at Emmy who was suddenly the last real, colourful, wonderful thing to see. All else was nothing, a frightening emptiness, like the beginning, or more likely the end of the world.

It roused itself and struggled up. It remembered faces of people like this Emmy, a mother, a father, a big brother, a baby brother, and it didn't want to say goodbye to them, not yet, not for a long time. And if it let that last bit of emptiness surround it, that's what would happen.

"What do I have to do?" it cried.

Emmy tried to put its arms on the real ghost's shoulders.

"I've been telling you, en' I? All this time, I've been tellin' you!"

The real ghost looked up. There was the red button. Even Emmy was beginning to fade, and that frightened the real ghost more than she thought it was possible to be frightened.

"You're going!" the real ghost said, alarmed.

"Not if you don't want me to. There's still time!"

The real ghost watched in sadness as Emmy

153

faded until she was barely visible.

"I can still see you," the real ghost said.

Emmy's eyes were full of tears, but also full of a desperate determination.

"But I'm goin'," she said, "I'm goin'. Unless you snap out of it. And you can, you have to!"

The real ghost felt the strength of the girl called Emmy. It tried to stand.

It failed.

It tried again.

It stood.

"I can hardly see," it said.

"Thas alright!" said Emmy. "There ain't nuffing here to see. You wanna see the real world again? You can. You must. You will. Do it!"

The real ghost tried to stretch up, but its body was limp and tired and it could hardly move.

"Are you sure you can't do it for me?" it asked.

Emmy's voice was distant now, hardly to be heard.

"I can't do nuffing," Emmy said. "This is you. Only you. You got the strength, I know you 'ave. Look at me!"

The real ghost looked into Emmy's fading eyes and still saw that incredible determination. But as she looked, the eyes blanked out, covered by the creeping emptiness that was upon it.

"Where are you?" the real ghost asked, anxious.

No answer.

It looked around.

There was only a faint redness above her, and that was fading, too. In a second, it wouldn't be able to see it and its last link with the girl and with hope of life would be lost.

It stood, it stretched, it cried, it screamed, it lifted its arm, it swung back its hand, it aimed and with a shout of triumph that filled the nothingness as if a new universe had been created from the bleakest void, it roused its aching heart, shook its sinking soul and smacked the red button with all its ...

20 Race

"**M**ight be an interesting little battle," said Mrs. Sumner, gently. "You two ready?" They were. "Well then, may the best girl win."

Emma Chandler and Emmy Fairchild lined up against each other in the fifteen hundred metre national school championships final.

A year had passed, six months for Emma to recover, six more for her to once again reach top gear.

Emma had been desperately hurt, her body needed time to mend and she had to learn simple movements all over again. She did, and Emmy helped her every step, literally, watching her friend recover even from injuries the doctors thought might never heal. When standing, Emmy stood with her; when walking, Emmy walked with her; when jogging, Emmy jogged with her and once she was running, Emmy ran with her. She couldn't have lived if Emma hadn't recovered, so there was never a question of 'if', only of 'when'.

At the same time and with no less attention, Emma watched over Emmy. She saw what no one else saw, or wanted to see, how Emmy's life had been squandered in poverty and aimlessness. There was no way Emmy was going back to her father and Emma would not let her parents consider anything other than adopting her. They objected – too risky, too expensive. There were discussions with a dozen different groups, but no matter what was discussed, Emma's well being came first and everyone could see that Emma wanted

Emmy around.

Not just around. Emma wanted Emmy to flourish. She was far too generous to let her remain as she had been and insisted on good schooling, as much help as Emmy needed, back to basics and then on to the stars.

Mr. and Mrs. Chandler had been apprehensive, to say the least, but they couldn't argue against their own daughter's recovery.

They agreed.

And they never regretted it.

Emmy proved as rewarding a daughter as Emma, and as impressive a student. Impressive was the word. She studied every free moment, learned to read in weeks and, once that hurdle was mastered, read every book in the house and most of those in the school library. For months she said little, just soaked up learning as if there never could be enough of it, and there never could be.

She changed, as mightily as any body, soul and mind could change in a single lifetime.

She felt that countless lights had been turned on in her head. She was astonished at how much there was to learn, and decided a whole lifetime wasn't enough to understand the world, the universe and the human heart. What had been her early life receded into the mists of time, a history that she thought about with sadness, but still with love – for she both loved and pitied the girl she had been.

Her father was out of prison, but didn't argue to get her back. Selfishly, he wanted some of the good things that had come her way, and got some, at least enough to keep him out of his daughter's life, but never enough to keep him out of trouble.

They spoke once a month.

"How are you, Em?"

"I'm fine, dad. I'm doing well."

"Getting airs and graces are you?"

"Dad, don't be nasty. I'm no snob. Neither are they. Be kind for a change."

Mr. Fairchild didn't see what kindness had to do with life. Life was still hard, always had been, always would be. You took what you could in any way you could, that was the name of the game.

As for Victor, he was locked up and would stay locked up. He joked and laughed at life, but the laughter was cruel, and he remained the man he had been, just less imposing now that Saul was dead.

The thought of the two men still scared the girls when they recalled that terrible day, but gradually the memory of what happened faded and they felt more secure. They would never forget completely, but the healing power of time didn't allow fears to hold them back for long.

Mrs. Sumner had given no thought to Emmy Fairchild as a runner. Emmy had kept her light under a bushel; only Emma knew how bright that light could shine and gradually persuaded Emmy to let others see it. For the first few months, Emmy had hardly run at all; she spent all her time attending to Emma. She made a promise never to run again until and unless Emma ran, too. She still struggled with guilt, and it was Emma herself who, with her kind and generous spirit, seemed most able to free Emmy of blame.

It dawned on each of them surprisingly slowly just how fast the other was.

"You're good!" Emma had said. "You're really

158

good!"

Once they knew the other's speed and strength, the spectre of a real race loomed, but they avoided the subject until it was impossible not to mention it, especially as the media built it up to the race of a lifetime.

Fifteen hundred metres, school watching, parents watching, the nation watching. After the accident, and for weeks after her recovery from coma, Emma had been front page news and in the hearts of the nation. That had faded as she recovered, but here she was again, with flashlights from newspaper reporters bursting around the stadium, not to mention television cameras here, there and everywhere. Neither she nor Emmy wanted to be celebrities; celebrity just plonked itself on them and they did their best to ignore it.

"You mustn't let me win," Emma had said, knowing what Emmy was thinking.

"Your mum and dad will hate me," Emmy replied.

"They'll deal with it," said Emma. "I think they're surprised at how much they like you."

"Then I'll hate me...myself. I don't think I can do it, Emma. Race without me."

"No!" Emma insisted. "I'm back to normal, you know that. The way I was. It's got to be a proper race. You have to do your thing, Emmy. You can't change what you are to please others, it won't work. You've got to come out of that shell for good, Emmy! Come out and be a butterfly!"

Emma might have had the excuse, if she came second, that the accident had affected her permanently. A lot of people who loved her would say that. But she knew differently. She was healed, completely. She felt strong and fit and full of life again. The weeks in coma and the months recovering had strengthened her, shown her just how fortunate she was and just how precious life was. Going on fifteen she knew what she wanted to do. She wanted , in one way or another, to heal people as she'd been healed. She'd needed Emmy to help her recover and she'd seen how Emmy herself had changed with love and care. That's all it took, nothing special. She felt something burn inside her that hadn't been there before, a bright light that Emmy, the accident and the long recovery had lit. She felt better than ever and knew, if she lost, that Emmy was simply better than her.

When Mrs. Sumner said "May the best girl win", neither of them thought the 'best' girl would win. There was no best girl, just two fabulous girls given the gift of gods.

The school, though, and the world beyond the school, were passionately divided.

Emma was the school's natural heroine, but Emmy was its adopted heroine. Banners in the stadium were spread half and half. It was much the same in the watching world, people finding reasons for their choice – either the miraculously healed or the mysterious healer. The competition might have split them, but instead it brought them closer together.

Emma was thrilled to be running again. More than thrilled, she was proud and jubilant, win or lose; Emmy was astonished that she'd come so far in so brief a time, not a mile, but a million miles. Emma had no regrets that she'd taken the train to London that fateful day; Emmy wondered what might have happened if Emma hadn't come, where they would be now and if anything or anyone had made it happen. Emma remembered the coma, how real it was, and how Emmy had entered her mind when no one else had been able to; Emmy thought about the weeks at the hospital and the secret, silent talks with her hurt and sleepy friend.

When the starter's gun fired, they let Jessica Willard make the pace. She led for two laps, hoping to tire the girls out, but neither of them tired and they overtook Jessica, stretching away themselves, breathing easily and revelling in the freedom of running, the wind in their hair and the rhythm of the race, in perfect harmony.

Until the final bend.

Metres ahead of the rest, they turned to look at each other and laughed, because although life was often nasty, brutish and short, it could also be a quiet revelation of kindness, goodness and love.

"Competition is competition," said Emma. "We can't fix it."

"No," said Emmy. "We mustn't."

"Not important, though, is it?" Emma asked.

Emmy shook her head. "Hope not," she answered.

"Right," said Emma, "on the count of three. Ready?" Emmy was ready. "One…" said Emma.

A pause.

"Two …" said Emmy.

Another pause.

"And three!" they called, together.

Acknowledgements

Special thanks to Carole and Rowel Samuels and to Peta Rudduck for reading the various drafts, suggesting improvements, encouraging and being generally generous with their time and energy. Also, thanks to Lulu for giving the silenced writer a voice, or at least a whisper.